KU-797-164

LITTLE
HORROR

LITTLE HORROR

DANIEL PEAK

Firefly

First published in 2021
by Firefly Press
25 Gabalfa Road, Llandaff North, Cardiff, CF14 2JJ
www.fireflypress.co.uk

Text copyright © Daniel Peak 2021

The author asserts his moral right to be identified as author in
accordance with the Copyright, Designs and Patent Act, 1988.

All rights reserved.
This book is sold subject to the condition that it shall not, by way of
trade or otherwise, be lent, re-sold, hired out or otherwise circulated
without the publisher's prior consent in any form, binding or cover
other than that in which it is published and without a similar condition
including this condition being imposed on the subsequent purchaser.

All characters in this publication are fictitious and any resemblance
to real persons, living or dead, is purely coincidental.

A CIP catalogue record of this book
is available from the British Library.

1 3 5 7 9 8 6 4 2

Print ISBN 978-1-913102-51-7
ebook ISBN 978-1-913102-52-4

This book has been published with the support
of the Books Council of Wales.

Typeset by Elaine Sharples

Printed and bound by CPI Group (UK) Ltd,
Croydon, Surrey, CRO 4YY

*For Amelia and Cara, who made
me think parts of this story might be true*

1

Prize Chimp

What's the first thing you remember?

Was it your first day at school?

Maybe your third or fourth birthday party?

The day you learned to swim or ride a bike?

Or when you lost your first tooth?

Not me. I don't remember any of those things, for one very good reason: they haven't happened yet.

But I remember some other things. Like the time I set fire to an ice-cream van. And the time I jumped out of my bedroom window in the middle of the night. I remember the time I broke into someone's house through the cat flap, and the time I tried to steal a Porsche 911 Carrera S. I'll tell you about all of those things, but I'll start with the very first thing I remember. Something that happened when I was seven months old.

That was a year and a half ago.

The very first thing I remember is lying on a plastic mat, with my bare bum sticking up in the air. Mum was holding my ankles with one hand, and wiping my bottom with the other one. I don't mean she was wiping my bum with her hand. That would be disgusting. She was using a baby wipe, and she had a fresh nappy all ready to slide into place.

But Mum wasn't moving. She was frozen mid-bum wipe, staring down at me with this weird expression on her face, like something spooky had just happened. I wondered what she had seen in my poo that had scared her so much.

'Say it again, Rita,' said Mum. '"Quarter to three." Say, "quarter to three"'. Without taking her eyes off me, she shouted Dad into the room. He came in a few seconds later, tapping away on his phone and not looking up.

'What's up?' said Dad.

'Rita just told me the time,' said Mum. 'I was chatting away while I changed her nappy, and I happened to say "I wonder what time it is" and she looked me straight in the eye and said "quarter to three".'

Dad pressed something on his phone. 'More like twenty to three I'd say.'

Mum looked annoyed. 'That's hardly the bloody point, is it, Paul? The point is this girl's seven months old and she's just said the words "quarter to three". Doesn't that strike you as a little bit weird?'

Dad shrugged. 'Not really. Babies make all kinds of noises. They sound like words sometimes. I had her in the park yesterday, could have sworn she called me a prize chimp.'

Mum gave Dad a strange look. Then turned back to me. 'Prize chimp,' she said. 'Rita, can you say, "Daddy's a prize chimp"?'

'Becky, she's a baby. If she could talk that would make her some kind of freak.'

Mum kept staring at me. 'Daddy's a prize chimp,' she said.

I kept my mouth shut. I could have said something but I didn't want Dad to think I was a freak. So instead I made some random ba-ba-ba noises then put my big toe in my mouth and started chewing it. After a while Dad wandered off with his phone and Mum carried on changing my nappy. She must have thought she'd imagined it all.

Should I have been honest? Should I have told Mum and Dad I could talk? I don't know. If I *had* told them, what happened next would have been very different.

2

Bucket of Wee

If you'd told my mum and dad that they had an amazingly, fantastically intelligent child, they would probably have agreed with you. But they wouldn't have meant me. They would have meant my brother, Lewis.

Lewis is two years older than me, and no one has ever called him a freak, so I used to watch him to see how normal children are supposed to behave. If Lewis shoved Lego up his nose, I shoved Lego up my nose. If Lewis tipped a bowl of spaghetti shapes over his head, I tipped a bowl of spaghetti shapes over my head.

And Lewis was handy for getting me out of trouble. Like when I completed a 200-piece jigsaw all by myself, or when I switched the telly over from CBeebies to the History Channel to watch a documentary on Cleopatra, Mum and Dad always assumed Lewis had done it. They thought he must be a child genius and so they bought him tons of educational toys, like a globe and a telescope. Poor Lewis wasn't interested in them, but I was. I used to spin the globe round and round, pretending to enjoy the shapes and colours when really I was learning the names of all the capital cities.

Another useful thing was when I worked out how to get subtitles up on the TV. That's how I learnt to read. As soon as I realised that the shapes at the bottom of the screen were the same as the things the people were saying, all I had to do was watch as much telly as I could – and that's pretty easy when you've got my mum and dad. It took me about three months to learn to read. I'd done it by the time I was one.

Writing was harder. I tried to teach myself using a set of crayons and some scrap paper but whenever an adult came near I had to scribble over everything I'd done so they couldn't see it. That made it hard to tell if I was getting better.

And there were other things to learn of course, like crawling and then standing up and then walking. I did those things at about the same age as normal babies. Potty training took a while. At the age of eighteen months, I could read and write as well as a grown-up, but I still sometimes pooed on the carpet if I didn't have a nappy on. Well, I never said I was perfect, did I?

I had lots of chances to tell my parents the truth. All I would have to do is pick up a jar of baby food and read the ingredients out loud. But I decided not to, for two reasons.

Reason number one: I didn't want Mum and Dad to drop dead of a heart attack.

Reason number two: people don't hide things from babies. When adults are with other adults, they're always pretending to be nicer and cleverer and more hard-working than they really are. But when they're with a baby, they stop pretending. Like, when Dad was with other adults he never trumped. But when it was just him and me in the kitchen, he would let rip with these long wet farts, then take an elaborate bow and go 'Ladies and gentlemen, I thank you', in a posh voice like he was proud of it. Sometimes he'd close his eyes and wave his hands through the air as the fart came out, like he was conducting an orchestra. But then if Mum came in the room and smelled it he'd go: 'that was Rita'.

Let me tell you a fact: when babies get blamed for a bad smell, five times out of ten it was their dad. And the other five it was their mum.

Here are some other secrets I found out:
- Dad told everyone he was too busy to watch TV or films, but really he watched *Inside Out* three times and cried at the bit where Bing Bong dies.
- One time when Mum changed my nappy, she put the very tip of her little finger in the poo and dabbed it on her tongue.
- Our window-cleaner sometimes wees in his bucket and then wipes the windows with it.
- Dad smokes cigarettes.
- Our local vicar kicks his dog.
- Kath, who is in charge at nursery, eats baby food for her lunch.

None of them are really amazing secrets, are they? It would have been nice to find out that Mum was a superhero, or that Dad secretly had a beautiful singing voice. But no, I find out our windows are washed with wee.

The point is, I didn't make any of those discoveries by sneaking around or spying on people. They just happened right in front of my eyes.

So I stayed quiet, to see what else I could find out.

I did tell some other people about my secret. I told other babies. Three days a week Mum took me to Funkytots nursery, where there were lots of other pre-schoolers. And at weekends we went to parks and soft play centres full of other kids. Whenever I met someone new I would talk to them to see if they were as smart as me. I'd wriggle over and whisper, 'Hi. Very pleased to meet you. I was just wondering whether you're as clever as me. Can you read? Can you write?' I'd look into their eyes for a little catch of understanding. Nothing. They just stared back, or dribbled, or poked themselves in the ear with a spoon.

It looked like I was on my own.

3

Nine Nine Nine

One other person knew.

Well, two people if you include my brother Lewis. Lewis saw me do grown-up things all the time but that wasn't a problem because no one listened to anything Lewis said. He would say, 'Daddy, Rita put new batteries in my torch' and Dad would just go, 'That was very helpful of her'. No one ever thought he might be telling the truth.

The other person who knew was called James and he was much more dangerous.

I met James when I was nineteen months old. It was after bath, and I was in my sleepsuit, on my playmat, picking out the *In the Night Garden* theme on a toy keyboard when Mum said, 'Look who's come to see you, Rita. This is James.' I looked up to see a messy-haired grown-up boy. All grown-ups look the same to me – old – but I guess this one was about fourteen or fifteen.

James gave me a big smile and knelt down next to my playmat. 'She's gorgeous, isn't she?' he said. Then he pinched one of my cheeks between his finger and thumb and wobbled it about. I hate it when people do that. No one ever does it to grown-ups because they'd probably end up getting a smack in the face.

James picked up my toy keyboard and started playing it himself while Mum called Lewis through and told him to put his listening ears on for a serious talk.

'Mummy and Daddy have to go out for a little while tonight, so James will be babysitting to make sure you're OK. OK?'

Lewis nodded. He didn't look bothered at the idea of Mum and Dad leaving him. They could have been off to start a new life on the planet Mars and he wouldn't care.

Mum turned to James. 'We're putting a lot of trust in you James, but I know you're very mature, and you got twelve predicted nines at GCSE so you're obviously an intelligent young man.'

'I love kids, Mrs Jeffrey. We'll have a blast.'

'Hm. Well I'll put them to bed before we go so you should have no trouble. But if there's anything at all you need to ask, my number's on the pad.'

Then Mum took Lewis upstairs for teeth and stories. As soon as she was out of the room, James ignored me. He went through to the kitchen and I heard bottles clanking. Then he came back through, talking on his phone.

'I'll text you when they've gone,' he was saying. 'But yeah, there's loads of vodka and stuff. They won't notice.'

James looked round the room. He saw Mum's bag on the end of the sofa. 'Ring you back,' he said, then ended his call and listened for a moment at the bottom of the stairs. We could hear Mum reading *The Gruffalo* and she was still only on the fox part, so James opened the zip of Mum's bag and took out her purse.

I could tell I was witnessing another secret moment. James opened Mum's purse and pulled out the paper money. Then he changed his mind, stuffed it back in and slid out the plastic cards instead. I knew what the plastic cards were from seeing Mum in shops and on the phone. The cards had special numbers on them that were the same as money. James took Mum's writing pad and copied down all the numbers from the front and back of the cards. Then he put the cards back in Mum's purse.

James looked over to see me watching him. He smiled again. 'They're only paying me twenty quid to babysit,' he said. 'Got to make it worthwhile somehow, haven't we, Chubbychops?'

I liked him even less now. To be honest, it wasn't so much the stealing as the Chubbychops comment. So what if I was chubby? I was nineteen months old. You try keeping the weight off when you're fed four times a day and the only exercise you get is at a soft-play centre.

A few minutes later Mum came back down to take me to bed. As she changed me into a night-time-nappy and put me down, I thought about what James was doing and I got more and more angry. Mum had trusted him – was *paying* him – to look after her house and her children, and he was going to invite his friend round, drink Mum's drinks and steal her money. It wasn't fair.

Mum kissed me on the forehead and went downstairs. I heard her telling James how the baby monitor worked, then saying goodbye and driving off to meet Dad from work. It was quiet for a bit, then I heard James talking again, back on the phone to his friend. The friend was probably on his way over here right now. I didn't want to let this happen, but how could I stop it?

Easy: I could make a phone call of my own. I could ring the police and tell them what James was up to. The police wouldn't know how old I was over the phone. They'd think I was a grown-up with a squeaky voice. And I knew there was a phone next to the bed in Mum and Dad's room.

The only problem was, I was stuck in my cot. It had tall wooden sides and I hadn't learned how to climb out. Someone would have to get the phone for me.

'Lewis!' I hissed. I tried to be as quiet as I could but still be heard across the landing in Lewis' bedroom. 'Lewis!'

He heard me. A few seconds later Lewis padded into my room, trailing Peter Penguin behind him. Lewis looked dopey. I must have woken him up.

'Lewis,' I said. 'Go in Mummy and Daddy's room and get the phone. Yes? Bring me the phone. But *don't make any noise.*'

Off he went. James had finished his phone call downstairs and it had all gone quiet. I started to worry that he would come up. What if he needed the toilet or something?

Lewis came back in to my bedroom with a phone. Not Mum and Dad's phone but one of those toy phones with a smiley face that you drag along on wheels. I sighed, annoyed. 'Not that phone, Lewis. The real phone. The one next to Mummy's bed.'

Lewis frowned at me. 'That's not allowed,' he said.

Great. Suddenly the boy decides to behave himself. I tried another way. 'We're going to phone Father Christmas. So you can tell him what presents you want.' Lewis' eyes lit up like fairy lights. It was the middle of April but that made no difference to Lewis. He was obsessed with Father Christmas all year round. He went back to Mum and Dad's room, and this time he did bring the right phone through.

'Good boy, well done.' I was going to ring the police myself, but then I had a better idea: get Lewis to do it. I'd seen a show on TV where a little kid had rung 999 when his grandma fell down the stairs. So it was believable that Lewis might do it, especially as Mum and Dad already thought he was super-clever.

'Now I want you to dial nine nine nine, Lewis. Can you do that? Do you know which button is nine?'

Lewis looked at me like I'd asked him to build a helicopter. Totally clueless. How Mum and Dad could think this boy was a genius was beyond me.

'Never mind,' I said. 'Give it to me.'

Lewis handed over the phone. 'Ring Father Christmas?' he said.

'That's right, Lewis,' I said, tapping in 9-9-9. 'I'll talk to him first though, OK?'

Only then did I notice James the babysitter standing in the doorway.

For a few seconds James said nothing. Then he said, 'What the…?'

I panicked. How long had he been standing there? How much had he heard? Perhaps if I acted like a normal toddler he would think he'd made a mistake. I started chewing the end of the phone and making baby gurgles.

'You spoke,' said James. 'Just then, you spoke.'

'Ba-ba ba-ga.'

'That's rubbish. You talked. I heard it all over that baby monitor.'

Oh bums, I thought. I'd forgotten about the baby monitor. James must have heard everything.

'She's ringing Father Christmas,' said Lewis, unhelpfully.

At that moment, my phone call was answered. 'Nine nine nine. What's your emergency?'

I didn't say anything. James was still staring at me. I didn't know what to do.

'Hello,' said the phone. 'Do you need help?'

'No thank you,' I said, and hung up. I looked at James.

'OMG,' he said. 'What are you? You can't be a real baby.'

'I am a real baby,' I said. 'I'm slightly advanced for my age. That's all.'

James looked at Lewis. 'What about him, is he a freak too?'

'Leave him out of it,' I snapped.

'Where's Father Christmas?' asked Lewis. This seemed to convince James that Lewis was normal after all, and he turned back to me. He stepped closer to my cot, but still not very close. I realised that James was a bit scared of me.

'One of two things, I reckon,' he said. 'One: alien life form. Two: government science experiment.'

I wasn't enjoying this conversation. For all I knew, one of James' guesses might be right. Perhaps I *was* an alien from space.

'Who else knows about you?' he asked. 'Do your mum and dad know?'

I didn't reply.

'They will,' said James. 'Everyone's going to know. I can sell this information to a newspaper. I can be famous.'

Things were getting worse. I felt so stupid. If I'd just kept quiet and gone to sleep in the first place none of this would be happening. What could I do to get myself out of trouble?

'If you tell people about me, I'll tell them about *you*,' I said. 'I'll tell them you copied the numbers off my mum's money-card.'

For a split second James looked worried. Then he smiled. 'I haven't used the cards yet. Anyway, I think people will be more interested in a freaky talking baby, don't you?'

James turned to go.

'Stop!' I called. I was desperate. I decided to tell

some massive lies. 'If you tell anyone about me, you'll regret it.'

James stopped in the doorway. 'What do you mean?' he said.

'I mean,' I said, making it up as I went along, '...what if I *am* a space alien? If you cause trouble, I could have you ... zapped, by a ... spaceship. I could have you blown into a million pieces. I could have you ... eaten by ... space ... lobsters.' I was talking total poo, and my squeaky, little-girl voice sounded far from threatening to my own ears – but it seemed to work on James. He sneered at me like he wasn't frightened, but I could tell that he was. 'Go back to bed, you,' he told Lewis. Then he took the phone off me and went downstairs. I waited a few minutes then, to be sure I'd got my message across, I pressed my face against the bars of the cot, as close as possible to my baby monitor and screeched into it, 'We'll be watching you!'

I heard James ring his friend to cancel the party, and after that there was no sound from downstairs until my parents got home. For a few days afterwards I was worried that James would tell someone about me, but it never happened. I went through Mum's address book and memorised

19

James' address and phone number in case I ever needed to get in touch and threaten him with space lobsters again, but it wasn't necessary.

James never came back to babysit again. I think Mum and Dad asked him, but he always thought of an excuse to say no.

And my parents never found out what had happened. Well, that's not true. They did find out, in a way. A few days later I heard Lewis talking to Dad in the kitchen.

'Rita had a fight with James and he said she was a alien. And Rita got cross. And Father Christmas was on the phone.'

'That's nice,' said Dad. 'Now come on, eat your Cheerios.'

4

Tiptoes Hits Funkytots

I thought my secret was safe. I thought I was the cleverest one-year-old on the planet, and that the cleverest thing I'd done was to stop anyone else finding out.

But I was wrong. A few months after the incident with James, someone else found out. And this person was far more threatening.

I found out about the danger I was in one morning at Funkytots nursery. Kath, the person in charge (the one who secretly ate baby food for her lunch) came in all excited and told the kids we had to behave very well this morning because we had 'a very special visitor!'

I was pretty excited. So were some of the other kids – the three- and four-year-olds who understood what Kath was saying. We hoped it might be Mr Tumble or a Disney Princess. 'Let's all give a big Funkytots hello,' said Kath, 'to Tiptoes the clown!'

I had never heard of Tiptoes the clown, and judging from the disappointed looks on the other kids' faces, they hadn't either. The door burst open and in came a man in a purple wig, full face-paint and a big red spongey nose. He had a bicycle horn in one hand, a big wooden clacker in the other and a whistle in his mouth. For a few seconds he stomped about making lots of noise. It was quite annoying.

'Hello everyone!' cried Tiptoes. He knelt down in front of a three-year-old called Ryan Cosgrove. 'What's your name, little girl?'

'I'm a boy,' said Ryan Cosgrove.

'Anna ... Boyd?' said Tiptoes.

'I'm a *boy*!' shouted Ryan.

'Great,' said Tiptoes. 'Come on then, Anna, show me where you keep all your dollies.'

For the next half an hour, Tiptoes honked and clacked his way around Funkytots, spending a few minutes with every kid, including me. He had a big painted smile on his face, but he never actually did anything funny, which seemed a bit weird for a clown. He tripped over his shoes a few times, but this seemed to really irritate him, so I don't think he was doing it on purpose. It's like he wasn't really a clown at all.

And then the visit was over. Tiptoes waved goodbye to everyone and left, tripping over his shoes again as he went. I remember thinking what a strange person he was. My group of one-year-olds was with Rachel in the Dolphin Room, and she told us it was almost time to snuggle down for naps.

And then Tiptoes suddenly walked back in.

'Excuse me,' he said, in a normal, not-clowny voice. 'Rachel, isn't it? I'm sorry to be a pain, but I'd really love a souvenir of my visit here. I wonder if you could join your colleagues for a photograph outside.'

'Oh,' said Rachel. She looked unsure. I could tell she wanted her photo taken, but she wasn't allowed to leave us alone without a member of staff.

'Don't worry about the kids,' said Tiptoes. 'I can watch them while you have the photo. It'll only take two minutes.'

'Erm ... OK,' said Rachel. She grabbed her coat and checked her makeup in the mirror bit of a Fisher Price activity centre, then nipped out to join the others. Nine toddlers were left alone with Tiptoes the clown.

Tiptoes looked at us. For the first time since he'd got here, he stopped smiling. He just stared at us like he was looking for something hidden, like we were a difficult wordsearch.

Then the smile came back. 'Hands up who likes ice cream!'

No one moved. The smile vanished again. 'OK, I give up,' he said. 'Which one of you is it? Who's the smarty-pants?'

We still didn't move.

Tiptoes plucked off his spongey nose, revealing a thin, pointy real one underneath. 'I know it's one of you,' he said, 'and I'm going to find out who, so it's better you tell me now.'

I knew he was talking about me and I was suddenly very frightened. I tried not to show it.

'What do you know about my project?' he demanded.

I didn't know what he was talking about, but I couldn't tell him that without revealing that I was the smarty-pants.

'Where are Vani Patel and the others?' he asked.

I still didn't know what he meant.

'For God's sake, you're one year old! You can't even walk straight. How the hell do you think you're going to escape from me?'

Daisy Croft started crying. Tiptoes got down on all fours and looked into her eyes.

'Is it you, cry baby? Hm?' He moved on to Jessica Barber. 'What about you, tough girl?'

Tiptoes was working his way through the room, looking into each child's eyes, searching for a spark of understanding. It was the same thing I'd done myself months ago and found nothing. What would Tiptoes see when he got to me?

Tons of other questions piled into my head. How had Tiptoes found out about me? How did he know I went to Funkytots? Why was he so interested in the first place?

I tried to push all the questions back out of my head. Tried to keep my eyes as blank as possible. I could think about this stuff later. Right now, the important thing was to look like a normal one-year-old.

My turn. Tiptoes stared right into my eyes. 'What about you, Fatso? Any little confessions to make?' I could smell the sweat coming through his face-paint. What should I do to look normal? I thought about tweaking his nose, but I was too scared to move.

Tiptoes moved on to stare at Katrina Brooks, but he had to stop then because Rachel came back in. Tiptoes instantly popped his nose back on and snapped back into his friendly old self.

'Excellent stuff!' he said. ''Fraid I made one little girl cry. I sometimes have that effect on women, ha ha ha. Well, thank you, everyone. I'll see some of you again, very, very soon.'

Seconds later Tiptoes was gone. He hadn't identified me, I was sure of it. I relaxed a tiny bit, and all the questions slid back into my head.

Rachel shuffled her coat off and spoke to us all. 'Right. Who needs a bottom change before nap time?'

We all did.

5

The Search

I was desperate to find out what was going on. Who was Tiptoes the clown? How did he know about me? Why was he out to get me? My own parents didn't know how smart I was, and yet somehow this scary clown seemed to know everything.

Had James the babysitter told him about me? But that didn't make sense. If that had happened, Tiptoes would know my full name and where I lived. There would have been no need for him to go to Funkytots and frighten all the other children. It was all too confusing. I couldn't work it out by myself and there was no one I could ask for help.

Or maybe there was. Whenever Mum and Dad had a question they couldn't answer, they would always do the same thing: check on their phone.

What's the weather going to be like tomorrow? Check on your phone.

How long will it take us to drive to Ikea? Check on your phone.

What do we do about Lewis' nits? Check on your phone.

What time is the party? Check on your phone.

'Check on your phone' seemed like the answer to all of Mum and Dad's questions, so maybe it could help me too. If I could get one of their phones, maybe it would tell me about Tiptoes the Clown.

But how could I get my hands on their phones? I had already tried to borrow them a few times, but Mum and Dad hardly ever put them down. The one time I had managed to grab Dad's phone, it came up with a message saying 'Use touch ID or enter passcode,' and I couldn't get it to do anything. Turns out you need the person whose phone it is to press their finger on the main button before it will work.

So I had given up. But now, with a crazy clown out to get me, I was determined to give it another go.

Mum put me down in my cot at the normal time and I lay there awake, waiting for my parents to go to bed. Once they did, I waited a bit longer until I was pretty sure they were both asleep. Then I climbed out of my cot.

It wasn't easy climbing out. I had to pile all my teddies on top of each other, then climb up the pile without toppling it. Then I hooked my arms round the top of the cot and tipped myself forward so I somersaulted over, landing on my back on the bedroom floor. Then I had to jump to my feet and run across the room to turn off the motion sensor on the baby monitor so it wouldn't beep in Mum and Dad's room.

When that was done, I quietly snuck across the landing and into Mum and Dad's bedroom. They were both asleep and snoring, with their phones lying on the little sets of drawers next to the bed. Dad was nearest, so I picked up his phone. I pressed the main button.

'Use touch ID or enter passcode.' This was the dangerous bit. Very carefully, I reached into the bed and took hold of Dad's hand, trying not to wake him up. I uncurled his pointy finger and pressed it against the button on the phone…

It worked! The phone lit up with lots of squares and pictures. I slid Dad's hand back into bed with him, then took the phone through into my room.

It took quite a while to figure out how the phone worked. I'd never used one before so I didn't know what most of the squares meant. One of them brought up a weather forecast, one of them brought up photos of me and Lewis, one of them brought up a map and one of them brought up a calendar. None of that was any help to me.

But then the phone brought up a box saying 'search'. There was a space where you could type in words. I tested it by typing in 'Funkytots Nursery', and up came lots of pictures and information about my nursery.

Good. Now I understood how a phone could tell you things. So I typed in the things I wanted to find out about. First I typed in 'Tiptoes the clown'.

Not much came up. There was a picture of a clown called Tiptoes, but he wasn't the Tiptoes I'd met, and he was from somewhere in America. So that hadn't taught me anything. But then I thought about it. It *had* taught me something: whoever he was, Tiptoes was not a real clown.

Next I put my own name in. Again, nothing helpful came up.

I tried to remember what else Tiptoes had said to us that morning. He'd said something about his project, and he'd mentioned a name. Something Patel. Vani was it?

I had a guess at how to spell Vani and typed it in. Lots of information and pictures came up. There were loads of people with that name, all around the world. It was impossible to tell which one I should be interested in.

But Vani Patel was the only clue I had, so I started reading through all the information anyway, and looking at all the pictures, one after another after another.

I had been doing this for about an hour when a message popped up on Dad's phone: 'you have 5% battery remaining'. I sat back against my bedroom wall and sighed. I had run out of ideas. Outside, the night was quiet. I could hear an ice-cream van tinkling through the streets but nothing else.

What if I tried searching for different words together? Like Tiptoes + Patel. Or Funkytots + Vani. I tried a couple of these. Nothing came up.

Hang on – an ice-cream van? With its music on? At one o'clock in the morning? The sound was getting louder as the van turned into our street and came nearer to our house. I had a sudden horrible feeling that the van was coming for me.

Calm down, I told myself. How could anyone possibly know where I was? Tiptoes hadn't identified me at nursery. And I hadn't done anything suspicious since then. I'd just come home and gone to bed. OK, I'd been searching on Dad's phone, but they couldn't trace me from the phone, could they?

Could they?

I went cold. I had no idea how phones worked. What if people could somehow spy on them and trace it back to your house? I thought of all the things I'd just typed in: Tiptoes, Funkytots, Vani Patel. If Tiptoes the clown *was* spying on Dad's phone, he'd now know exactly who he was looking for. Me.

The ice-cream music stopped. Ten seconds later our doorbell rang.

6

Wendy

They had to ring twice before there was any movement in Mum and Dad's room. Then a third time, followed by some very loud knocking before Dad shuffled out of the bedroom shouting for whoever it was to keep their hair on.

Dad went downstairs and called out through the locked door. 'Who is it?'

'Police.'

A bit of a pause. Then Dad said, 'In an ice-cream van?'

'Open the door, sir. This is very important.'

'It's half one in the morning.'

'Open the door, Mr Jeffrey, or we'll have to force an entry.'

There was no doubt about it; they were here for me. Was I just going to sit in my bedroom and wait for them? I looked around the room. My Peppa slippers were in the corner, and my pink hoodie was hanging up over the back of my little plastic chair.

Downstairs, I could hear Dad pulling back the bolt on the door and looking through his keys for the right one. 'What's this about?'

'It's about your daughter,' said the voice.

'My *daughter*? She's one year old. She's asleep in her cot.'

I wasn't. I was standing on my windowsill, wearing my pink hoodie over the top of my sleepsuit and my Peppa slippers on my feet. I took one last look around the bedroom for anything else I might need. I thought about taking Dad's phone, but no, the bad guys might be able to trace it. What else should I take?

One thing. I jumped down and pulled Other Rabbit through the bars of my cot before climbing back up onto the windowsill.

I could hear Mum coming out of her bedroom. 'Who is it, Paul? What do they want?'

Dad called up, 'I don't know. Something about Rita.'

'About *Rita*?'

I opened my bedroom window and shuffled out backwards. The downstairs of our house is

34

bigger than the upstairs, so there's a bit of kitchen that sticks out. That was lucky because it meant I didn't have too far to drop. I let go of the windowsill and fell down onto the kitchen roof.

Next I had to drop down again, into the garden. It had been a drizzly day, so I knew the grass would be soft. But when I looked over the edge of the kitchen roof it seemed a hundred feet high. No way I could drop that far without breaking something.

I looked round for help. Dangling beneath me, next to the back door of the kitchen was a hanging basket. A few months ago it had had flowers in, but they'd all died and it was now just a pot of soil.

I lay flat on my belly, swivelled round, and lowered my feet into the hanging basket. It just about held my weight. Then it didn't. As soon as I let go of the roof, the little chains holding the basket snapped and I fell backwards onto the grass. I could have been hurt except that Other Rabbit cushioned my fall. Good idea to bring him after all.

The moment I landed, the big light went on in my bedroom, throwing a bright oblong across the grass. I ran into the shadows and squeezed along the side of the shed just in time to hear Mum screaming 'Where's Rita?' and to see a head appear at my bedroom window, looking out. It wasn't Mum or Dad's face but I couldn't tell more than that because it was in shadow. And I didn't want to hang around and find out.

I squeezed my way around the side of the shed, tucking my hands into the sleeves of my sleepsuit so I wouldn't get splinters. From the back end of the shed I could get into next door's garden, and from there through some broken fence panels into one of the gardens behind us. I ran down the side of that house and out onto the road.

Now what? It was the first time in my entire life that I had been out of the house on my own, and I didn't know what to do. The easiest thing was to run along the pavement, but that would be stupid. It didn't matter whether the ice-cream men caught me or not, *anyone* who saw me toddling down the road in the middle of the night would pick me up and hand me in to the police. Better to stay away from the road and keep moving through people's gardens.

I ran up a driveway to a gate. It was quite high but I thought I could get over it – until I noticed the big shiny picture of a snarly dog and the words, I LIVE HERE. Try next door instead.

There was a car parked in next door's driveway, so I climbed onto the bonnet, then onto the top of the wheelie bin, and over their gate into the back garden. As soon as I landed, a bright security light went on, and that started next door's Alsatian barking and scrabbling at the fence that separated us.

I ran on, behind a greenhouse and into another garden. The dog stopped barking, and I could hear the other sounds of the night. A motorbike engine, a far-away car alarm. And the tinkling music of the ice-cream van, back on the move. Was it heading this way? There was no time to stop and work it out. I had to keep moving.

I don't know how many gardens I scrambled through that night or how long I kept going. I remember that I knocked over a bird table and squashed a lot of flowers. One time I came face to face with a fox who looked at me for a little while before disappearing into the bushes. It felt like I went for miles and miles but it was probably only eight or nine streets. I kept going until I couldn't hear the ice-cream music any more.

I didn't know where I was. My sleepsuit was soaked up to the belly from wet grass and from falling into a fishpond. I had no strength to keep going and, even if I had, I couldn't tell if I was moving further or closer to where I'd started from. I had to find somewhere to rest until morning.

By now I was in a long garden behind a posh-looking house. You could tell that kids lived here because there was a basketball hoop and a big plastic tractor in the garden. And a Wendy House.

It wasn't exactly warm in the Wendy House, but at least there was a roof if it started raining. I took off my sleepsuit and laid it out to dry. I took my nappy off too and threw it away. Whatever happened from now on, there would be no one to change me. I'd have to make sure I didn't have accidents.

I curled up in a ball, zipped my hoodie round my knees and sat in the corner of the Wendy House. I wondered what was happening back at my house and what Mum and Dad and Lewis were doing now. Were they out looking for me? Had they called the real police? Where was Tiptoes?

What happened next was the most unlikely thing of the whole day. I fell fast asleep.

7

Paw Patrol

My house looked wrong.

It was early the next morning and I was standing on the other side of the street, looking across at the building where I'd spent every night of my life apart from the last one. As soon as it got light, I'd put my soggy sleepsuit back on, crept out of the Wendy House and slowly managed to find my way back home.

Because it was so early there was no one around apart from a couple of people out running and a lady walking her dog. Whenever I saw someone coming, I jumped out of sight into a garden or behind a parked car. I suppose there are some advantages to being small.

And now here I was, back on my street looking at my house. But this wasn't what I expected to see.

I expected there to be police cars. I expected maybe some yellow tape across the street and TV reporters talking to all the neighbours. I mean, that's what you get when a kid goes missing isn't it? Cameras, helicopters, stuff like that?

But's that not what I saw. The house was quiet. There wasn't a single person in sight. No yellow tape, no police, nothing. The only thing that looked different from yesterday was a wooden sign planted in our front garden: SOLD.

Carefully, I crossed the road and stretched up to ring the doorbell. It was too high, even when I jumped. So I knocked on the door instead. No reply. I walked around to knock on the window, and that's when I saw that something else was different. It was like the house had got bigger, less friendly. Then I realised: it was empty. There was nothing on the windowsills, the pictures had gone from the walls. There was no dinosaur mobile hanging from Lewis' ceiling.

My family had moved out.

I couldn't work out what was going on. All I knew was that bad guys were after me, that it had something to do with Tiptoes the Clown and an ice-cream van, and that the bad guys had somehow made my family disappear.

One thing was for sure: I couldn't stay here peering in through the window. There might be someone in there now, looking out for me, ready to grab me. Even if there wasn't anyone in the house watching, the day was getting lighter and soon the street would be full of people on their way to school or work. And here I was, a toddler, outside all by myself, clutching my toy rabbit. Someone would stop and ask me questions and take me to a police station. And then Tiptoes would definitely be able to find me.

Right now, I had to stay safe, look after myself and avoid getting caught. And that meant I had to do three things. One: get changed out of my soggy sleepsuit into something more normal looking. Two: get food and drink supplies. Three: find a place to hide out and give me time to work out what I should do next.

The change-of-clothes one was pretty easy. There's a family on my street with a little boy my age called Prayan. They've got a long washing line in their back garden and, luckily, they'd left a load of washing pegged up overnight, including some of Prayan's stuff. The washing was too high up for me to reach but, when I looked in their shed, I found some long-handled cutters like I'd seen my dad use for clipping bushes. I held the cutters up over my head and snipped through Prayan's family's washing line so all the clothes floated down onto the lawn. I thought it might leave a clue if I only took the toddler clothes, so I ended up stealing everything, including two beach towels and a pair of grown-up pyjamas.

I carried the fat bundle of washing a couple of streets away, where I could hide behind some big metal bins at the back of a car park. I looked through Prayan's clothes and picked out an outfit: a Paw Patrol T-shirt and an orange pair of jeans. I put them on. They fitted pretty well and I liked them. Mum and Dad always dressed me up in pink clothes with unicorns and cupcakes on them. Prayan's family had much better taste. I still only had Peppa slippers on my feet but they would have to do for now.

Mission one accomplished. The next thing was to get supplies.

8

Haribo Starmix

The only way to get supplies was the same way I got clothes: stealing.

I didn't like being a thief, but what else could I do? Even if I had money, which I didn't, I could hardly toddle into a supermarket and fill a trolley full of shopping. The staff would go nuts. No, I would have to steal it.

It was a short walk to the big Tesco near our house. The day was getting lighter now and there were more people about, especially when I got close to the main roads, but no one stopped to ask me who I was or why I was outside by myself. Maybe they didn't believe what they were seeing.

At the big front doors of Tesco, I hid behind the trolleys until I saw a man on his way in, reading a shopping list. As he went into the shop, I toddled along behind him. Anyone watching would have thought he was my dad. Then as soon as we were a little way inside, near the fruit and vegetables, I swerved off and started looking for my own supplies.

It was massive, this Tesco. I'm not just saying that because I am small. I mean it was a really enormous shop, the kind where you can buy food but also clothes and bicycles and lawnmowers and tellies and whatever. I knew that what I needed was food to keep me going now that Mum and Dad weren't around to cook for me.

The shop wasn't very busy, so I acted fast. I tucked the bottom of my hoodie into Prayan's orange jeans, zipped it halfway up and shoved loads of food inside. It is important to have a varied diet, so I stuffed milk chocolate and white chocolate and Smarties and Skittles down there, and topped it off with a box wrapped in plastic called 'Deluxe Assortment'.

When I couldn't fit any more supplies down my top, I turned to go – and saw someone watching me.

It was a boy, about two years old. He was staring at me in silence, the way little kids do when they watch someone else being naughty. His tongue was poking out, licking the snot on his top lip back and forth like a windscreen wiper. I slowly backed away, just as his mum appeared round the end of the aisle.

'Come on, Finn. Let's go and find the teacakes.'

The boy didn't move. 'That girl took the sweeties,' he said.

That's when the mum noticed me. 'Oh. Hello, love,' she said. 'Where's your mummy?'

I could see where this conversation was heading and I didn't like it. Best to get out of here as quickly as possible. I turned and ran up to the other end of the aisle. As I ran, my hoodie came untucked from my jeans and six bags of sweets skittered out across the floor.

I ran all the way back to the shop entrance and tucked in behind a woman with a full trolley on her way out to the car park. I followed the woman, just as I had done on the way in. It looked like I'd got away with it…

Wrong! As soon as we stepped outside, the alarms on the doors started flashing and beeping. A man in a shirt and tie stepped out to block the woman's path. He looked at the woman, then looked at me and saw the 'deluxe assortment' of chocolates poking up out of my hoodie.

The shirt man spoke to the woman. 'Would you and your daughter please step back into the store for a moment.'

The woman looked confused. 'Daughter?'

The man and the woman both looked at me. I threw the box of chocolates at them and made a run for it out towards the car park, but when they saw me running towards the moving cars they both panicked and ran after me. I felt the man's hands on my shoulders and I was lifted up and carried back into the shop.

The man set me down and looked at the woman suspiciously. 'You're telling me this girl isn't yours?'

'I've never seen her before in my life.'

'Whose is she then?'

'I don't know, do I? Ask her.'

The man turned his attention to me. He got down on one knee to be nearer my height, and smiled in quite a kind way, though he still kept a tight hold on my shoulders. Then he said, 'Hello sweetheart. Where's your mummy?'

I said nothing. I did my best impression of a

frightened toddler. Not difficult really, since that's what I was.

'My name's Tim,' said the man. 'I'm a security guard here. Tell you what; let's see if there's some sweeties in my office while we find your mummy and daddy. OK? You come along with me.'

Forgetting all about the woman, Tim took me by the hand and led me past the checkouts to a door with a keypad on it. He tapped in a number and pushed the door open. I tried to see what the door code was but it was too high. Tim led me down a corridor to a small office and sat me on the desk. From here it was going to be harder than ever to escape.

At least he'd been telling the truth about the sweeties. Tim tore open a bag of Haribo Starmix and put it on the desk next to me, then picked up a microphone and spoke into it. 'This is a customer announcement. If any parent has lost a child in store, please make yourself known to a member of staff immediately. Thank you.' He clicked off the microphone and smiled at me. 'We'll have you back with mummy and daddy very soon.' I imagined Mum and Dad coming through the door to pick me up and take me home. Yeah, dream on.

On the desk behind me was a TV screen flicking between different parts of the shop. In a few minutes, when no one came to collect me, I knew Tim would start rewinding the screen to look for clues. He'd see the film of me ten minutes ago, coming into the store and wandering about on my own. Then what? I'd probably get handed over to the police, and if that happened I was sure Tiptoes would find out about it and come to get me.

I had to escape from Tesco now. But how? First, I had to get rid of Tim. I tugged at my jeans and jiggled my bottom up and down on the desk, trying to make it look like I needed a wee-wee.

Tim got the message. 'Right,' he said. 'Erm … OK. Can you hold it for just a minute, sweetheart? I'll go and get someone.' He left me sitting on the desk and went out of the office, shouting for someone called Maggie.

I didn't have much time. Quickly, I grabbed a piece of paper and a pen and wrote a note: *Thank you for finding my little girl. I was so worried! Yours sincerely* – and I signed it with an unreadable scrawl.

Not exactly a great plan but the best I could come up with. Grabbing Other Rabbit and the rest of the

Haribos, I slid off the desk and ran out of the office into the corridor, turning in the opposite direction from Tim. All I wanted was a door to the outside world or even a small window to wriggle through, but it felt like every turn took me deeper into the heart of Tesco, further away from freedom.

I managed to push open a heavy door and stepped into a huge cold room with a hard stone floor. It was like being in another supermarket, but one with much higher shelves, stacked with cardboard boxes, tins and jars, all wrapped in thick rolls of plastic.

I worked out that this must be a storeroom, where they keep all the supermarket stuff before it goes onto the shelves. I heard a sudden loud hissing sound and saw a lorry reversing. Behind it was a big open gateway onto the world outside. I wanted to make a run for it, but there were three Tesco people there waiting to unload the lorry. How was I meant to get past them?

The driver climbed out of his lorry and started eating a sausage roll while the Tesco people pulled boxes of out of the back and stacked them up on a wooden trolley.

'Last drop?' asked one of the men.

'I wish. Still got Morrisons and Waitrose. Any returns for us?'

'Just the blue crate over there.'

I watched them from my hiding place behind the shelves. Standing still was making me twitchy. Tim would have got back to his office by now, found me missing and read the note. He'd be looking for the woman who'd written it. I had to act now, do whatever it took to get past those men at the lorry. I looked around for ideas – and saw a knife lying on the floor. The Tesco people probably used it for opening cardboard boxes and cutting the plastic wrappers off things.

I picked up the knife. It had a heavy metal handle with a button that made the sharp bit slide up and down. I thought about how I could use it. Deep breath. I held the knife tightly and stepped out towards the men.

Three seconds later, Tim ran into the stockroom. 'Excuse me, lads. You've not seen a woman lately?'

Someone laughed. 'Anil's not seen a woman since two thousand and six.'

'I'm serious. With a little girl, about two years old?'

'No one's come through here, mate.' I think it was the driver talking, but it was hard to tell. By then I'd crawled inside the blue plastic crate.

I heard Tim leave, and then the floor dropped away from me as someone lifted my crate, carried it to the back of the lorry and loaded it on. There was a thundery clatter as the shutters on the back of the lorry were pulled down, and half a minute later we were on our way. At first I tried to concentrate on the movement of the lorry to work out which road we were on, but I soon had to admit I had no idea. The important thing was to get off the lorry before we started driving down the motorway or I could end up hundreds of miles away.

I climbed out of the crate into the gloomy space in the back of the moving lorry. I crawled across to the edge. That's when the knife became useful. I slid out the sharp bit and stabbed it through the rubbery curtain stretching along the side of the lorry. I dragged the knife along, ripping a slit through the material. Then I lay on my belly and peeked out at the road speeding past. As soon as the lorry stopped at traffic lights I wriggled my legs out through the slit, took a deep breath, screwed my eyes tight shut and dropped down onto the road, twisting my ankle as I landed. I scrambled to my feet and limped as quickly as I could across the pavement and up a grassy slope to hide behind some trees. Back down on the road, the traffic lights changed and the lorry hissed and drove away.

I felt terrible. My mission to get supplies had been a disaster. I had nearly got caught and all I had to show for it was half a bag of Haribo Starmix. And now here I was, lost in the middle of nowhere, with hardly any food and no idea where to go or what to do next.

Then I realised where I was. And I had a brilliant idea.

9

Ball Pool

I'd escaped from the lorry a few miles away from Tesco in a part of town with no houses. Instead there were some brick buildings with not many windows and lots of car parking spaces outside. One of the buildings was called a 'timber merchant' and another one was called '24-hour gym'. I hadn't been in either of those so I didn't know what they were. But I had been in the next building, lots of times. It was called Rumpus and it was a soft-play centre.

What better place can you think of for a one-year-old girl to blend in?

It must still have been early in the morning because Rumpus wasn't open yet. I had to spend an hour wandering around the car park, sucking on the Haribos to make them last as long as possible before someone arrived to roll up the big metal shutters.

Getting in was easy. I just followed the woman who'd opened up. As she was shrugging off her padded coat and switching on computers, I crawled past the front counter on my hands and knees, under the turnstile and into the cavernous play area.

Rumpus looked weird at this time of day, with no children in it. It looked wrong. It reminded me of my empty house. I looked over my shoulder to make sure the lady was still busy with her computers then I scrambled up a ramp as quietly as I could towards the highest, darkest corner of the play frame.

And that's where I waited. After about half an hour, a few kids had arrived with their parents and started tearing around the place so I decided it was safe to come out from the shadows and join in. It felt strange being there on my own, without Mum or Dad or Lewis, but once I was zipping down the slide and squeezing between the big squidgy rollers I almost forgot about my problems and started enjoying myself.

I thought Rumpus would get boring after a few hours, but you know what? It didn't. I went on the big slide at least two hundred times, and I swung round and round the spinning poles until I was dizzy. All the running around made me hungry, and I'd only had half a bag of Haribo Starmix to eat since yesterday, but even that was fine because Rumpus had a café bit where people could buy sandwiches and bowls of chips, and it was pretty easy to sneak bites of food off people's tables when they weren't looking.

And none of the staff or parents noticed that this little girl was here all alone. My guess had been right: at Rumpus I was just another tiny face in the crowd. As long as I wasn't having a tantrum or puking up in the ball pool, no one paid any attention to me.

The problem came at closing time. Half an hour before Rumpus shut, a voice came over the speakers telling all customers it was time to leave. Mums and dads started climbing onto the play frame to gather up their sweaty kids. Some of the children didn't want to leave and ran squealing back up the ramps. The parents followed, getting cross, but this only made the kids more excited.

While all this fuss was happening, I climbed back into my dark corner at the top of the frame.

I sat with Other Rabbit and listened to the noises of the last kids being scooped up and dragged away, some of them crying for one more go on the slide. I waited, not moving. I heard the staff collecting money from the till and putting it into bags, and a bit later heard them saying goodnight, going outside and locking the doors.

The building looked deserted. I decided it was safe to come down. I started walking down the ramp, then changed my mind and went head first down the biggest bumpy slide. You're not allowed to go down head first, but now there was no one around to tell me off. I shot to the bottom and landed with a cloppity noise in the ball pool at the bottom.

It was fun, and I was about to climb up and do it again when I saw a movement over near the café. There was someone there! A grown-up! I looked for the nearest place to hide and decided the best thing was to burrow down out of sight under the plastic balls.

Stupid idea. I was hidden away out of sight, but wriggling down there made the balls rattle against each other. The grown-up was bound to hear me.

And yet the person, whoever she was, didn't

come over. Instead she kept walking round the café bit. Through a gap in the balls I could see her going back and forth from table to table, wiping them. Of course: a cleaner. But why hadn't she heard me rattling around in the ball pit? As I kept watching, the cleaner seemed to be dancing. She *was* dancing. She had little wires going into her ears, the same as Dad had when he watched films on his phone. That's why the cleaner hadn't heard me: she was listening to music. I was safe, as long as she didn't come over to clean out the ball pool.

The next hour was very uncomfortable. I lay in the pit, covered up with plastic balls, like a prize in a lucky dip, hoping the cleaner wouldn't come over. It was fine; she didn't. She hoovered the carpets and wiped a cloth over some of the play frame but that was all. Lucky for me she wasn't a very good cleaner.

When she'd finished, the cleaner switched off the lights and let herself out. I heard her pull down the metal shutters which told me that now I definitely was on my own. I climbed out of the ball pit into the dark, empty play centre. I had the place all to myself until it opened up again tomorrow morning.

First I found the main light switches. I dragged a chair across so I could reach them, and I switched everything back on. Then I walked over to the café bit and had a look round behind the counter. There was a big fridge full of sandwiches, crisps, yoghurts and a plastic box full of fruit. I opened the fridge and had my dinner, washed down with a Fruit Shoot and six Freddo bars for pudding.

Then I had a look round the building. There wasn't much that I hadn't already seen. I walked into the boys' toilet just because I could. I went into the party room where they have the food and cake on people's birthdays.

Off to one side of the main play area was a door that said 'staff only'. Through there I found another toilet, an office with a computer and a slightly bigger room with a kettle in it. This must be where the staff came to have their lunch. There were some newspapers lying on the table, so I had a look through in case one of them mentioned the case of a missing one-year-old girl called Rita Jeffrey. None of them did.

One of the newspapers had a section that said: 'Got a story? Call our 24-hour hotline and leave a message. We'll call you right back.' I had a story all right, but I didn't want to share it with any grown-ups, not yet. Still, I memorised the phone number in case I needed it in future.

For a few minutes I thought about using the computer in the office to see if I could find out more information about Tiptoes the Clown. But I knew that would be stupid. Last time I tried that, the ice-cream van came after me. I had learned my lesson. No more phones or computers.

So I did sensible things instead. I found a lost property box and picked out some clothes that fitted me. If I was going to be living here for a while, it would be a good idea to change my appearance a little bit every day. Next I finished exploring the building, working out where the exits were in case I had to leave in a hurry.

After that, I went back into the toilets and had a wash, soaping myself up from the squirty dispenser thing, then standing under the hot air from the hand dryer. I didn't have toothpaste or a brush, so I swooshed tap water round my mouth and spat it into the sink.

And then there was nothing left to do except wait for tomorrow. I switched the big lights back off, then took Other Rabbit back across the dark floor of the play centre, climbed the ramps to the top level and found the same spot where I'd hidden that morning. I dragged together some foam blocks to make a mattress, climbed on top and pulled a lost-property coat over myself as a blanket.

And the next day? Was the same, only more boring. I hid from the staff, I played on the slides for a few hours, I stole bits of food from tables in the day and I had a big meal at night. I checked the newspapers to see if they mentioned me or my family, but they didn't.

It was the same the next day and the one after. The only thing that changed from day to day was that the cleaner would hoover a different bit of carpet and I would have different sandwiches for dinner. For the first few days I worried that the staff would start to recognise my face and realise that I was there every single day, but they never did. I was just another kid.

I nearly got into trouble on day five. I was crossing the rope bridge for what seemed like the millionth time when I heard woman's voice say 'Rita?'

I looked down to the main area and saw Ryan Cosgrove's mum, from nursery. 'Hello Rita! I heard you've not been in nursery all week. Have you been poorly?'

I did the shy kid look. 'Where's your mummy and daddy?' asked Ryan's mum. 'Are they in the café?'

I ran on across the rope bridge and kept well out of sight for the rest of the afternoon. When I finally had a proper look round, Mrs Cosgrove had gone. I decided to look more closely at the people around me. I didn't want to meet any other adults who might recognise me.

How long could I have carried on living like that? Weeks? Months? I sometimes think I could have spent years growing up in Rumpus until one day, when I was about ten or something, I could just step back out into the world as a normal person and live a normal life. Then I wouldn't be a freak any more.

But that's not the way things turned out. Because on my ninth day in Rumpus, everything changed.

10

Day Nine

Day nine began like every other morning in Rumpus. I woke up, I waited for the shutters to roll up, I waited in a corner until enough children arrived for me to join in. Like every other day I played a bit, climbed and slid and spun, and like every other day I stole food at lunchtime.

It must have been the school holidays because Rumpus was busier than usual. And there were older children here, the age that would normally be in school. So the whole place was a bit more boisterous. There were kids climbing *up* the bumpy slides (against the rules), throwing balls out of the ball pool (also against the rules) and there was more crying and screaming than usual. I didn't mind. The busier it was, the easier it was to stay unnoticed.

One boy in particular seemed to enjoy

terrorising kids smaller than himself. And since he was about ten years old and built like the mammoth from the Ice Age films, kids smaller than himself meant pretty much everyone in Rumpus. I watched as he deliberately knocked over a little girl trying to climb the scramble net, then trod on the fingers of a boy crawling out of a tunnel.

I know I should have ignored the kid. But I couldn't. For the last nine days I had been stuck in Rumpus, feeling more and more angry with the people who had broken up my family. I couldn't do anything to hit back at them, but I could do something about this ten-year-old bully. So I did. I put myself right where the kid could see me.

Sure enough, the nasty little bully soon picked me out. I had put myself at the top of the bumpy slide where one hard shove would send me flying down backwards. It was too tempting for him to resist. He came charging towards me. It was easy for me to skip out of the way so he fell and belly flopped forwards onto the slide.

But I hadn't finished with him yet. As the boy fell, I grabbed his ankle to stop him sliding away. He looked up at me as if to say thanks, then saw the carton of apple juice I had in my hand. I smiled at the boy. 'Everyone's going to think you weed yourself,' I said, squirting the whole cartonful over his pants. Then I let go of him, watching him squelch and slide backwards down the slide crying for his mummy as he went.

It was at that second, when I was feeling the most pleased with myself, that a small hand clamped over my mouth and I was dragged suddenly backwards, away from the top of the slide and into one of the see-through tunnels that runs through the Rumpus play frame.

The hand let go and I turned to look at who had grabbed me. It was a little boy wearing shorts and a stripy jumper. He looked about a year older than me.

'Are you Rita Jeffrey?' said the boy. 'I've been looking for you! Pay very close attention: you're in terrible danger and you don't have much time!'

11

Mr Close

I couldn't speak. I didn't know what to say. After nearly two years of pretending to act like a baby, here I was, finally face to face with someone like me, and all I could do was to stare at him like a dozy toddler.

'I am right, aren't I?' said the boy. 'You are Rita? You go to Funkytots nursery and the ice-cream van came to your house and you escaped and…'

'Yes,' I interrupted. 'That's me. How do you know all that? And who are you?'

'My name isn't important,' said the boy. He was an odd-looking kid. He had bright yellow hair but with black tufts in it, like he'd had paint dripped on him. It made him look like a leopard. 'The important thing,' he said, 'is that you get away from here as quickly as possible.'

'Get away?' I spluttered. 'I'm not going anywhere.

I want to know what's going on. What happened to my mum and dad and brother?'

'I'm afraid Mr Close has got them,' said the speckle-haired boy.

'Mr Close?' I said. 'I've never heard that name in my life. Who is he?'

'He's the man who's got your family,' said the boy.

This conversation was going round in circles. 'OK,' I said. 'So he's a bad guy. But who is he? What does he want? And how do you know about him?'

The boy looked a bit embarrassed. 'I know about him,' he said, 'because I'm one of his children.'

'You mean … he's your dad?'

'No! I mean I'm one of the children in his facility.'

'Facility?' I asked. 'What's that?'

The boy sighed, like all this should be obvious. 'It's the place where smart kids like us come from.'

This was getting even more confusing. 'But I didn't come from a facility,' I said.

'No,' admitted the boy. 'And that's what makes you special, and it's why Mr Close is so desperate to get his hands on you. You're the only one of us ever to pop up in the outside world. And that's why you're the only person that can help us.'

'What do you expect me to do?' I asked.

'Go to Vani Patel.'

I knew that name. Tiptoes the clown had said it back at Funkytots. 'Who is Vani Patel?' I asked.

'She's one of us. Three years old. She was raised in the facility, and she's the leader of the only team ever to escape.'

'And where do I find her?'

'If Mr Close knew the answer to that, he'd already have caught her. What we *do* know is that one of her crew was spotted four days ago in Bramwell Gardens.'

I knew Bramwell Gardens. It was a big park a few miles away where Mum and Dad would sometimes take us for picnics and to see the fireworks on bonfire night. The kind of park that has swings and slides but also a big old house in the middle and an ice-cream kiosk and a lake with rowing boats.

'But why don't you go and find Vani Patel?' I asked.

'Impossible,' said the boy. 'I can't get away from Mr Close.'

I sat up very straight, shocked. 'You mean he's here?'

'Of course,' said the boy. 'He's been looking for you for nearly two weeks, going round all the centres and playgrounds. Adults aren't allowed in without kids; that's the reason he brought me here.' The boy turned and pointed down to the café area. 'That's him: brown jacket, eating a muffin.'

I looked down at where the boy was pointing and saw Mr Close. A thin man wearing glasses, sitting on his own.

And I recognised him. His outfit was different of course, and he wasn't wearing face paint. But I knew that I was looking down at Tiptoes the Clown.

I shuddered in fear. Not because I'd recognised him, but because he was already standing up from the table, pushing his glasses up his pointy nose and heading over towards the playframe.

And then he looked up at the see-through plastic tunnel, and he looked straight at me.

12

Rumpus

Mr Close smiled, as if I was already in his grip. I was too scared to move. Mr Close kept smiling up as he walked towards the ramp and started climbing.

'Excuse me, sir!' A member of staff in a green Rumpus T-shirt tapped Mr Close on the shoulder.

'What?' snapped Close. 'I'm going to collect my kids.'

'Not with shoes on you're not. No shoes allowed on the play frame.'

Annoyed, Close tried to undo his shoes. He didn't want to take his eyes off me, so he made a bad job of it, hopping on one foot as he picked at the lace. This was my chance to get away. I flipped onto my belly and started to slide backwards out of the see-through tunnel.

Something stopped me. I looked up. The

speckle-haired boy had grabbed me by the hood of my top.

'Get off me!' I yelled. 'I need to escape!'

'You forgot something,' said the boy. He handed me Other Rabbit.

I nodded my thanks. 'What's your name?' I asked.

'George,' the boy replied. As I slid backwards out of the see-through tunnel, dragging Other Rabbit with me, George winked. 'Good luck, Rita.'

I peeked over the top of the play frame, looking for Mr Close. There was no sign of him apart from his pair of shoes abandoned at the bottom of the ramp. That meant he must be somewhere climbing his way up towards me. I looked for the fastest way down: the bumpy slide. I raced to the slide, only to see Mr Close crawling over the top of the scramble net like a spider. At that same moment, Mr Close saw me, and with one heave he was up and over, lying on his belly just inches away from me.

'Come on, Rita darling,' he smiled. 'Time to go home.' There were other adults around but they just thought Mr Close was my dad coming to collect me. I shoved my way past the other kids and threw myself headfirst onto the slide. Down I zipped until...

Whumph. Halfway down I slid into the back of a tubby dad, bum-shuffling along in slow motion with a burbling toddler on his knee.

'Careful there, sweetheart,' said the dad. I climbed across onto the next lane of the slide, but Mr Close was already at the top, pushing kids aside and jumping on. I turned round and tried to climb back up my lane of the slide but it was too slippery. Mr Close was now shooting towards me like a rocket. He stuck his arm out to grab me as he sped past, but I dodged back behind the bum-shuffling dad, and Close missed. A second later he was at the bottom of the slide, waiting for me.

'Come on, Rita,' he called up. 'Don't be scared. Daddy's got you.'

I was trapped. Couldn't go up, couldn't go down.

But I could go sideways. One good thing about living in a soft play centre for nine days is that you get to know where all the short cuts are. I knew there was a big rip in the netting at the edge of the slide, so I scuttled across to it like a crab and wriggled through the gap, onto an in-between level of the play frame.

Mr Close saw what I was doing and he didn't look happy. He started climbing back up the ramp to get me. What could I do now? There was another slide running down from this level, a twirly tunnel slide, just the right size for a nearly two-year-old girl and the wrong size for a grown man. In I went, just as Mr Close appeared on my level.

As I sped out of the bottom of the slide, still clutching Other Rabbit, I knew I had a chance. For the few seconds it took for Mr Close to get down the twirly tunnel slide, he couldn't see me. This was my moment to escape. I couldn't go through the front entrance because Rumpus don't let kids leave without adults. I'd have to get out through one of the other doors.

I plucked my shoes from the shoe pouch. Then I had an idea and I grabbed Mr Close's shoes too. He wouldn't be able to chase me so easily in just his socks. I ran through one of the 'staff only' doors, past the little office and hurled myself with all my weight on the door that said 'emergency exit'.

13

Keys

I spilled out into sunshine and fresh air, away from the dried-wee smell of little children for the first time in nine days. I could hear alarms whooping behind me. It must have been one of those doors that sets an alarm off when you open it. Good. Hopefully the alarm would cause lots of chaos in Rumpus, and that might help me to escape from Mr Close.

George the speckle-haired boy had told me to go to Bramwell Gardens. But how was I meant to get there? I sort of knew where Bramwell Gardens was, and I could probably find my way there, but whenever Mum and Dad took us we went in the car, and even that took about twenty minutes. It would take hours to get there by walking.

I looked at the buildings surrounding Rumpus. Alongside the timber merchant and the gym, there was a place for getting your car fixed and one that sold 'soffits and fascias', whatever they are. Then there was a car-washing place with two men in fleecy tops sponging down a taxi. Behind them, six sparkling cars were lined up waiting for their owners to return.

I threw Mr Close's shoes into a bush and ran over to the line of cars. The men with sponges didn't notice me as I stood on my tiptoes and looked in the window of the first car. I knew that cars wouldn't go unless you put a key in the little slot next to the steering wheel. It was too much to hope that any of these cars would have keys in them, but I looked anyway.

And there was. There was a key in it.

I tugged on the door handle and it popped open. I climbed into the driver's seat, stretched my arms out and put my hands on either side of the big steering wheel. In the middle of the wheel it said 'Porsche'.

Of course I'd never driven a car before, but I had always watched carefully from my baby seat when Mum and Dad drove our car at home, so I thought I had a pretty good idea of how to do it.

By now lots of people were coming out of

Rumpus. That's what you do when an alarm goes off: you evacuate the building. I could see them all by looking in the mirror sticking out from the car door. I couldn't make out Mr Close but he would be there somewhere, looking for me.

Time to get out of here. I reached my feet down for the pedals. But even at the longest stretch of my little legs it was hopeless. Either I could put my feet on the pedals or I could look out of the front windscreen. Not both.

OK, fine, so I would make do without seeing out of the window. The main thing was to get out of here, even if I bashed a few trees on the way. I wiggled the sticky-up thing like Mum always did. Then I turned the key and the engine roared awake. I tried to move the stick to where it said R for 'reverse' so I could drive it backwards out of the car park. But the stick wouldn't move.

Try the pedals instead. I wiggled my bottom off the seat and stood on the pedals one by one. One of them made the car roar even louder, but it still didn't go anywhere.

What was I thinking? A tiny girl trying to drive off in a stolen car? It was stupid. I'd have crashed before I got out of the car park.

I peered back out of the window, over to Rumpus. No one in the small crowd of people seemed to be paying attention to my car. But the men at the car wash were. They were already running over to find out who was trying to steal their Porsche.

I opened the car door, jumped out and ran away across the grass as quickly as I could. Behind me I heard a voice shouting 'Oi!' but I didn't stop until I was safely out of sight behind another building. This one was called 'Get Mobile'. Inside, I could see an office with a frizzy-haired woman talking on the phone. Outside, there was a line of ten little buggies. Mobility scooters. The kind that old people use to go shopping.

Could I make my escape on one of these?

Unlike the Porsche, none of the scooters had keys in them. I looked back in to the office where the frizzy-haired woman was still on the phone. Behind her I could see a row of little keys on hooks on the wall. If I could get to those keys, perhaps I would have more luck with the scooters than I had with the car. But first I had to get that woman out of the office.

How? Easy. I ran past the scooters and found a

patch of grass where Frizzy-hair could see me through the window. Then I just sat down and started eating handfuls of grass. It didn't take long for Frizzy-hair to notice me. She looked alarmed. She checked to see if there was a grown-up with me and when she didn't see anyone she got up to come and fetch me.

As soon as she started moving, I got up and ran all the way around the outside of the building. That way Frizzy-hair would come outside, not be able to find me, and go off looking. And while she was doing that, I was running in through the open door of her office. I clambered onto her desk, reached up and just managed to tip one of the keys from its hook.

With the key in my hand, I ran back out to the scooters. The key didn't fit in the first scooter, so I tried the second one. This one sort-of fit but wouldn't turn. I moved on to the third scooter, glancing round to see where Frizzy-hair had gone. I could see her over at Rumpus, talking to people in the small crowd, probably asking if anyone had lost a little girl.

The third scooter wouldn't take the key, but the fourth one did. It made a whirry noise and some lights came on. I pulled a waterproof hood up over my head, pushed the start button and turned the wheel. The scooter started to move. And unlike in the Porsche, I could see and work the controls at the same time. Hooray for little old ladies!

Outside Rumpus, Frizzy-hair was talking to Mr Close, who was standing in his socks looking very upset, as you'd expect from a dad who'd lost his little girl and had his shoes stolen. Frizzy-hair was pointing to the place near 'Get Mobile' where she'd seen me sitting on the grass, and soon she and Mr Close were running over there to look for me. But they didn't pay any attention to the very tiny, hooded old lady sailing down the far side of the road on her mobility scooter.

14

Roundabout

They're good fun, those old-lady scooters. Even though I was on the run from the baddies, and even though an ice-cream van might zoom up and grab me at any minute, I still kind of enjoyed myself. The scooter probably wasn't as fast as a Porsche but it was good enough for me. The other useful thing was that none of the people driving past gave me a second glance. I don't think I look like a little old lady, but when you're in a mobility scooter, under a rain cover, people just see what they expect to see. It's kind of like being invisible.

The fun stopped when the battery ran out. A little light started flashing, and a mile later the scooter just stopped dead and wouldn't start up again. I didn't know what to do so I just grabbed Other Rabbit, jumped off the seat and ran away, leaving the scooter abandoned in the road.

But by now I had nearly made it to Bramwell Gardens and I could cover the last little distance on foot. Instead of going in by the main entrance where I might have been spotted by adults, I found a narrow footpath alongside the fence and, after checking there was no one around, I pulled myself up over the top and dropped onto the grass next to some thick trees.

It was late in the day now. The trees threw out long shadows and there was a thin sliver of moon in the sky like a bitten-off fingernail. I probably only had couple of hours to find Vani Patel and her group before it started getting dark. And I didn't want to be in Bramwell Gardens on my own at night. Being alone in Rumpus was one thing: it was lonely there but at least it was warm. Here it would be cold and maybe wet, and there would be no fridges full of snacks to eat.

So I needed to find Vani Patel quickly. I was standing at the edge of an empty playing field. A couple of people were walking dogs, and at the far end of the field a bunch of grown-ups in coloured vests were doing press-ups on the grass while a man shouted at them. There were no kids around.

I walked along the line of trees until I came to

a small lake. The lake was quiet apart from two grown-ups out in a rowing boat. Beyond the lake was the main playground. I couldn't see it from here, but I could hear the screamy, squawky sound of happy children. Probably that was the best place for me to start looking.

I walked around the lake, past a closed ice-cream kiosk and a rubbish bin that hadn't been emptied for a long time. I looked at the overflowing cans and sweet wrappers and wondered how long it would be before I got my next meal. I wondered if I was hungry enough to rummage through the bin, or to pinch a slice of bread from that boy over there feeding ducks in the lake.

I looked again: that boy feeding the ducks in the lake. That boy, that little boy, all on his own. He looked about three years old. He shouldn't have been standing by a lake all alone at his age. And why were there no ducks anywhere near him?

I walked back over to the boy. He had mussed-up black hair and his clothes were grubby. As I got closer I saw that he wasn't feeding the ducks at all. He had a slice of bread in his hand, and he was making picking-and-throwing movements, but he wasn't actually throwing any of the bread into the water. Which explained why there weren't any ducks.

'Hello,' I said. The boy swivelled his eyes to look at me but he didn't reply.

I couldn't think what to say next so I asked him, 'Can I have some of that bread?'

'No,' said the boy.

'Right. Er. My name's Rita,' I said. 'I'm nearly two.'

'I'm three and a half,' said the boy. From the way he said it, I still couldn't tell if he was clever or not.

'I'm looking for Vani Patel,' I said.

The boy didn't react to the name. He kept pretending to pick at his slice of bread. I was about to say something else when he said. 'Roundabout. Ten minutes.' Then he threw the whole slice of bread into the lake and slipped away backwards into the bushes.

Ten minutes later, I went into the main play area. There were a few families around but no one seemed to notice I was on my own. Sure enough, the black-haired boy was there, standing next to the roundabout, waiting. I walked over to him.

'Get on,' said the boy. I got on. The boy pushed

the roundabout round five times to build up speed and then hopped on next to me.

Straight away I felt dizzy, especially with no food in my tummy. 'Can we talk somewhere else?' I asked.

'No,' said the boy. 'Has to be the roundabout. Three-hundred-and-sixty-degree vision. Excludes the possibility of surprise attack.'

My head was in a spin. If someone did try a surprise attack I wouldn't even be able to stand up straight. But I didn't argue with the boy.

'Who are you?' he asked.

'I told you. I'm Rita.'

'Who sent you?'

'No one sent me.' I suppose that was a bit of a lie since George, the boy from the tunnel at Rumpus, had sent me. But I didn't want to say anything that would make the boy mistrust me. 'I'm just like you,' I said. 'I'm a clever kid, a brainy kid, whatever, but I didn't grow up in your … facility. But Tiptoes the clown found out about me and the ice-cream men kidnapped my family and now Mr Close wants to get me. That's all I know, apart from there's someone called Vani Patel, and her group might be able to help.'

The boy looked at me for a few seconds. The roundabout started to slow down, so he got off and pushed it for a couple more spins before jumping back on.

'What else do you know?' he asked.

I thought about it. 'Nothing.' I was telling the truth now. I had told him everything I knew.

'OK,' said the boy. 'Go round the back of the toilets. Vani's waiting.'

The boy slid back off the roundabout and yanked it to a stop. I stumbled off, feeling a bit sick, and staggered around to the back of the toilet building. I looked around for Vani but there was no one there, just litter and some clumps of nettles. I turned to go back the way I'd come – and that's when someone kicked my legs, right behind the knees, making me buckle to the ground, and a heavy bag was pulled down over my head.

15

Bramwell Hall

I cringed under the bag, expecting something heavy to knock me out at any moment. But it didn't happen. And whoever had caught me, it wasn't Mr Close, or any other adult. From all the whispering, I was pretty sure it was kids.

I felt myself being lifted up and carried on four sets of shoulders, two at the front and two at the back. It wasn't too uncomfortable, except that the ones at the front kept dropping my feet on to the floor and struggling to pick me up again.

I decided to say something. 'I'm not going to run off or anything,' I said from inside the bag. 'If you put me down and take the bag off my head, I'll walk.'

This led to more whispering conversation, then a new kid's voice said, 'We'll put you down, but we aren't taking the bag off. We're taking you to a secret location.'

'OK,' I said.

The kids set me upright. One of them held my hand and led me on through scratchy bushes and across a slippery bit of mud. I couldn't see where we were going but from my memories of days out with my family I reckoned they were leading me to the big, empty house in the middle of the park.

Thinking about it, this was a bit disappointing. Until now I had hoped maybe Vani Patel and her group were a team of amazing superkids with a secret underground base full of computers where they'd protect me and help me fight to get my family back. But so far it seemed like they were making things up as they went along.

Then again, they *had* managed to escape from Mr Close's facility. And if they could escape, then maybe Mum and Dad and Lewis could escape too.

Those were the thoughts in my head as I was led through the mud, across more grass and onto a cobbly footpath. Soon we stopped and I heard the scrape of wooden boards being shifted. I felt someone press down on top of my head, forcing me to get onto my hands and knees and crawl forward through a low doorway. I waited on the other side and listened as more hands and knees shuffled through behind me. Then came the sound of boards shifting again as they closed the entrance.

And then the bag was pulled off my head. At first it didn't make much difference: it was pitch black in here. But then a torch went on, lighting up a big, bare room with stone floors. The kid with the torch walked around the room, switching on lamps. They were all shapes and sizes, from tall lamps to the kind of little bendy table lamp Mum had on her desk at home. Finally the kid got to a small electric heater and switched that on too.

The kid switched off the torch and I saw that he was the boy from the duck pond. There were three other children in the room, all about the same age as Pond Boy.

No one had said a word since we came in, so I did. 'Where's the kitchen? I'm starving.'

One of the girls reached into a plastic bag and slid some food towards me. A bag of Mini Cheddars and a pot of hummus skittered across the floor and hit my feet, followed by a rolling plastic bottle of water.

'Thanks.' I opened the Mini Cheddars and used

them to scoop piles of hummus into my mouth. The kids watched me, keeping their distance. The room was cold but I could already feel the electric heater plus five little bodies beginning to make the place more comfortable.

'I guess one of you is Vani Patel,' I said.

'I'm Vani.' It was the girl who had given me the food. She was the smallest person in the room, apart from me. She didn't look like the leader of a rebel gang, but I suppose not many pre-schoolers do.

'I think an explanation is in order,' said Vani.

'I think you're right,' I agreed.

And then we sat in silence for a few seconds. We were both waiting for the other one to do the explaining. I sighed. 'I'll go first, shall I?'

I opened the water bottle and took a swig. The label said 'fresh spring water' but that's not what it tasted like. I didn't want to think about where Vani had filled the bottle so instead I concentrated on telling my story. I told them about my life so far, about Tiptoes' visit to Funkytots and my late-night escape through my bedroom window. I told them about Rumpus and Mr Close and – well, basically I told them everything I've told you.

At the end, Vani and the others looked confused. Come to think of it, they had looked confused most of the time I was talking. When I finished, they just stared at me. 'Go on then,' I said. 'Your turn.'

Vani shrugged. 'What do you want to know?'

What a stupid question. 'I want to know *everything*. First, what happened to my family?'

'I don't know,' said Vani.

'Well, what about your families? Where are they?'

'We haven't got families. Only each other.'

'So when did you work out you were, you know, different from other kids?'

'We're not different,' said Vani. 'We're the same.'

This was getting annoying. 'OK,' I said. 'Just tell me how you ended up living all by yourselves in an empty mansion surviving on Mini Cheddars and pond water.'

So she told me.

16

Electric Fence

'There were twenty-seven of us in the facility, all roughly the same age. We grew up together, learned together, ate together, played chess together...'

'You didn't think it was weird for tiny kids to be playing chess?

'Is it?'

'Yes. It's very weird.'

Vani shrugged. 'It was normal for us.'

'What about your parents? Where were they?'

'We only ever saw one grown-up, and that was Mr Close.'

'But what about the ice-cream men?

Vani looked confused.

'Never mind. I'll stop interrupting. Carry on.'

'So, we played chess together and had lessons together. Mr Close said we were lucky, because he was a *good* grown-up. He was the only one we could trust. He said that if we ever saw another grown-up we should keep quiet and still, the same as if you came across a wild animal. Other grown-ups were dangerous: that was very important, that was lesson one.'

'But how did you never see anyone else? Were you locked up in a prison?'

'No,' said Vani. 'We lived in lodges, like most people.'

'Lodges?' I said. 'Most people live in houses or flats.'

Vani looked a bit annoyed. 'Lodges are like small houses. Kids don't need full-sized houses do they? We lived in little lodges on little streets.'

'With cars and buses and shops?'

'Well no.' said Vani. 'We *knew* about motor vehicles from our studies, but we never saw them. And there weren't shops either. Mr Close provided all the food and clothes we needed, and gave us our pills.'

'So where did the streets lead to?'

'They mostly went round in a circle or to the training grounds and the swimming pool. I'll show you a map if you like.' Vani nodded at one of the girls, who came over to me with a folded-up bit of paper. I took the paper, and the girl quickly scuttled back to her corner of the hall as if she was scared I might bite her.

I looked at the folded-up paper. I thought it would be a hand-drawn map but no, it was properly printed out on colourful, shiny paper. It was a bit faded, like it was a few years old, but it was still easy to read. Above the map it said, 'how to find us' and there were directions from the motorway.

I unfolded the paper. The front section said 'Forest Shades Holiday Village – Get away from it all in the splendour of ancient woodland,' above a photo of a family of four people and a dog, all running through a pile of leaves. Everyone in the picture was grinning, even the dog.

The other sections of the shiny paper showed the same family jumping into a swimming pool, ten pin bowling, riding bicycles and sitting round a table laughing at their food.

'I don't know who those people are,' said Vani. 'I think they must have left before we were born.'

I flipped the paper over. On the other side was a bigger map, showing the layout of 'Forest Shades Holiday Village.' Like Vani said, there were roads going around a lake, and some leading off to a 'sports academy' and a 'tropical aqua lagoon.'

'Where did you get this map?' I asked.

'William found it,' said Vani.

'That's me, I'm William,' said Pond Boy. 'I found it behind a fridge when I was on cleaning detail.'

I looked at the paper again. At the words on the front: *get away from it all.* 'These roads all go round in a circle,' I said. 'Didn't you ever explore the world outside the edges of the map?'

'We couldn't do that,' said Vani. 'There was a fence all around the edge of the facility. Three fences to be precise. The inside fence and the outside fence were about as high as two lodges. But the in-between fence was only a couple of metres. At first we didn't know what it was for, but then we started to notice that there were always dead animals lying next it. Squirrels and rabbits, things like that. They'd been electrocuted. You could see where bigger animals, like foxes and badgers, had burrowed in to try to get to the meat – and they'd been electrocuted too. There was even a dog one time. There was obviously a strong current going through that fence.'

'So you *were* prisoners,' I said.

'That's not the way Mr Close described it. He said the fence was for our protection, to stop grown-ups from getting in.'

'And you believed him?'

'Of course,' she said. 'Mr Close had looked after us our whole lives. He'd taught us everything we knew. Maths, grammar, science, ethics. We had textbooks too of course so we could study by ourselves.'

'What about the Internet?'

Vani looked at me. 'What's an Internet?'

'It's kind of … erm…' I didn't know what to tell her. How do you explain the Internet to someone who has never heard of it? To be honest, I didn't really understand it myself. 'The Internet is pretty complicated,' I said. 'Let's just say it's a way of finding things out without asking Mr Close. Plus it's a way of watching films and cartoons and stuff like that.'

Vani looked confused. 'What's films and cartoons?' she said.

What was going on with these kids? They knew how electric fences work but they'd never heard of cartoons. For the next few minutes I asked Vani loads of questions to work out what things they knew about and what things they didn't know about.

Things Vani's gang knew about: maths, science, Chinese, chess, very old books.

Things Vani's gang didn't know about: Netflix, Happy Meals, football, soft play centres, Paw Patrol, where they lived on a map of England, global warming, Haribo Starmix.

I was slowly building up a picture of where they'd come from. Growing up in an empty holiday village. Being held prisoner behind an electric fence. Learning only what Mr Close taught them. Not knowing anything about the world just a few miles outside.

'If it was me in that facility,' I said, 'I'd have escaped straight away. I'd have whacked Mr Close over the head with a brick, then tied him up with rope and then I'd have gone and found a switch to turn off the electric fence.' The way I was describing it, it sounded quite simple. Perhaps that's how Vani and the gang *did* escape.

But Vani was shaking her head. 'Impossible,'

she said. 'The prefects would never let us get away with it.'

Now I was confused again. 'Prefects? What are they?'

'They're children, same as us. But they're Mr Close's favourites. He took them aside for extra lessons, teaching them how to spy on the rest of us. I think he was teaching them how to beat us in fights as well. I'm not sure. I do know the prefects got better food and nicer lodges than everyone else, especially Hector.'

As soon as Vani said the word 'Hector', the other kids all seemed to shiver.

'Who's Hector?'

'Hector is the main prefect. He's Mr Close's chief spy. And he's the nastiest one too. Mr Close gave him special authority to punish us if we stepped out of line. He was allowed to cut our food rations or make us sleep outside in the woods. And because Hector liked punishing us, he'd try to trick us into doing things wrong. One time he made Hannah draw a rude picture of Mr Close.' Vani pointed to the scared-looking girl who'd given me the map. 'Hannah didn't want to draw it but Hector threatened to make her sleep outside for a week.

Then, when she did draw the picture, Hector left it in the house for one of us to find. The test was whether we would report it to Mr Close. If we did report it, Mr Close punished Hannah. If we kept quiet, Hector punished us all.'

'He sound horrible,' I said.

'He is,' said Vani. 'He's the meanest person I've ever met. Admittedly I've only ever met thirty people, but he's definitely the worst. In a way though, Hector helped us. It was his horrible behaviour that made us determined to escape.'

'So how *did* you escape?'

'One night there was a storm. A really vicious storm. It caused a lot of damage in the facility.'

I remembered that storm, a few weeks ago. I'd been at home, curled up safe and warm in my cot. It felt like a lifetime ago now.

'The next morning, all lessons were cancelled. Mr Close put us to work patching up leaks and clearing the branches that had fallen across the roads. Some solar panels had come loose from the roofs and blown into the trees, so we had to find and retrieve them. It was all very chaotic and for the first time in ages it felt like Hector wasn't watching us too closely. I was in the forest, near the boundary fence and that's when I saw it. A tree had been hit by lightning.'

'The tree knocked down the fence!' I said. 'That's how you got out!'

'Not quite,' said Vani. 'If the fence had been down the electric circuit would break and Mr Close would know about it. This tree was half-fallen. Some of its roots were still in the ground. But the way it fell against the fences made a sort of bridge. I knew if we climbed it we could get over. So I ran back to the facility and found some people I could trust.' She nodded towards the other kids in the room. 'We climbed along the fallen tree, past the outside perimeter, and dropped into the field. It was a big drop but the ground was wet from the storm so it didn't hurt too much.'

'What was the other side of the fence?'

'A farm I think. The grass was very short and there were no animals, so I don't know what it produced. There were some holes in the ground with flags in.'

'That sounds like a golf course,' I said.

'What's a golf course?' asked Vani.

'It really doesn't matter. Carry on.'

'We ran across the grass, trying to get as far

away from the facility as we could. Soon we got to a huge wide road, with real cars on it, the first ones we'd ever seen, all going really, incredibly fast.'

'The motorway. Before you ask: it doesn't matter what a motorway is.'

'We walked along the edge of the fast road until we found a little bridge over the top. Then it was more fields, then a river. Then some more fields. Eventually we ended up here.'

'And then what happened?'

'What do you mean?'

'Did you go to the police, the papers?'

Vani looked at me. 'What's the police the papers?'

'OK.' I took a deep breath. 'Did you talk to *anyone*?'

'Of course. Once we were sufficiently far from the facility, we spoke to the first person we saw. We told him who we were and how we'd come to escape the facility. We even showed him the map.'

'What did he say?'

'Nothing actually. He just started crying and ran away.'

'Vani,' I asked, 'how old was this person?'

'I'd estimate approximately nineteen months.'

I sighed. 'Right. So what happened when you spoke to an *adult*?'

'We didn't speak to any adults.'

I couldn't believe what I was hearing. 'You mean, in all the time you've been free, you haven't approached a single grown-up?'

'Grown-ups are dangerous.'

'That's what Mr Close told you! But Mr Close is a liar!'

'Not so,' said Vani. 'Most of what Mr Close told us is perfectly true. And his first rule was always: don't talk to grown-ups. Grown-ups are dangerous. We haven't been given any reason to doubt that.'

'*Some* grown-ups are dangerous,' I said. 'Mr Close is the best example. But not all of them!'

This was so frustrating. But I couldn't really blame Vani and the others. After all, I'd been on the outside my whole life and I'd never told the whole truth to any grown-ups either.

'So all the time you've been free you've just sat around here eating Mini Cheddars and pretending to feed the ducks,' I said.

Vani looked a bit grumpy. 'We've been very

busy actually. Gathering food. Finding ways to keep warm.'

'And now what? Have you got any idea what you're going to do next?'

'Yes,' said Vani. 'We're thinking about going back to the facility.'

'Going back!' I yelled. 'Are you completely insane?'

'Well, what else can we do?'

'Here's what you can do: you can trust me. And I'm telling you that it's OK for us to tell some adults now. The time has come.'

'What if the adults are on Mr Close's side?'

I thought about this. It was a possibility. Could I be absolutely sure we could trust the police? It was impossible to know.

'OK,' I said. 'Here's the plan: tomorrow morning we'll split up into three groups. That gives us more chance of finding a grown-up we can trust. Vani and Hannah, you go to a police station. William and – you, the other girl – you go out and find the biggest group of grown-ups you can, and tell them everything. I'll go and find a newspaper office. Between all of us we'll get the story out.'

'But what if they don't believe us?' asked Vani. 'We haven't got any proof.'

'Haven't got proof?' I said. 'Look at us: we *are* proof! We're toddlers who talk like teenagers! All we have to do is open our mouths and the adults will have to believe us. Then we'll show them the map and they'll go to the facility, and Close will be arrested. And we'll see how he likes being locked up and punished.'

I was getting excited. For the first time since Tiptoes showed up at Funkytots, I felt like I understood what was happening and had some control over the situation.

Vani looked less enthusiastic. 'Are you sure this is the right thing to do?'

'I'm positive,' I said. 'This is your chance to rescue all your friends back at the facility.'

'I suppose so,' said Vani. But she didn't look very sure.

'What's the matter?' I asked.

'One thing is still bothering me,' she said. 'You were sent here by a boy you met at a … play place?'

'Play centre, yes. He said his name was George.'

Vani looked puzzled. 'We don't know anyone called George.'

That was odd. I thought back to the moment in Rumpus when the boy had grabbed my hoodie. There was a label on the inside of the neck. The label said 'George'. Had the boy given me a fake name? Why would he do that?

'Can you describe the boy you met?' asked Vani.

'He was a bit older than me,' I said. 'Pale white skin, with freckles. And he had a speckled pattern in his hair, sort of like a leopard.'

The atmosphere in Bramwell Hall changed instantly. The children stared at me in horror.

Vani said, 'The boy you met was Hector.'

17

Other Rabbit

'But … that doesn't make sense,' I protested. 'The boy *helped* me. He let me escape. Why would he let me escape if he was a baddie?'

'Hector must have had a reason.'

'Maybe he's secretly on your side after all.'

'Hector?' Vani almost laughed. 'No chance. Whatever Hector did, it was what Mr Close wanted. If Hector let you escape, that means Mr Close wanted you to escape.'

'No,' I said. 'Mr Close tried to catch me. He chased after me, but I was smart; I got away from him.'

'Remind us,' said Vani. 'How exactly did you get away from him?'

'Well,' I said, 'I went down a twisty slide. And then at the bottom, I stole his shoes.' At the time it had seemed like a daring escape, but re-telling the story now I had to admit it did sound a bit easy.

'Then I ran out a back exit,' I continued, 'and I found a car with the key in the starting-slot.'

'That was convenient, wasn't it?' said Vani.

'But I couldn't drive the car. So I stole an old-lady scooter instead.'

Vani didn't say anything else. She didn't have to. I had made my escape from Mr Close in an eight-mile-per-hour old-lady scooter. It was ridiculous.

But it still didn't make sense. 'Why would Mr Close let me escape?' I asked.

'I know exactly why,' said Vani. 'It was so you'd lead him to us.'

'But he already *knew* you were here. It was Hector who told me where to find *you*.'

Vani thought about this. 'He knew we were hiding out in Bramwell Hall?'

I thought back to what the leopard-haired boy at Rumpus had said. 'Not exactly. He said one of you was spotted in the gardens.'

'*One* of us,' said Vani. 'But Mr Close needed to find *all* of us, together, in the same place. And what better way to ensure we all got together in the same place than to send you along?'

'Are you saying Mr Close followed me here?

But he didn't. I'm sure of it. No one followed me. I came here totally alone.'

Vani walked up to me.

'Alone?' she said. 'No Rita. You didn't come here alone did you?'

And with that she plucked Other Rabbit from my arms and tore his head off.

18

Bugs Bunny

I got Other Rabbit as a present from Mum and Dad on the day I was born. They always said he was a present from big brother Lewis, but obviously it was Mum and Dad that bought him. I had lots of other stuffed toys, including another bunny almost as big as I was, but Other Rabbit was always my favourite. He came with me everywhere and as a result he was shiny and threadbare in places and covered in holes, and his head lolled over to one side.

So it was very easy for Vani to rip his head off. And when she did, it was easy to see the small plastic box that had been shoved down into his stuffing. Shoved down there by Hector when he had first grabbed hold of me at Rumpus. The box was smooth and white, with a tiny hole and flashing light on the top.

'What's that?' I asked.

'Tracking device,' said Vani. 'Tracking and listening, to be precise. See that little hole? That's a microphone. Not only does Mr Close know where we are, he's been listening to our whole conversation. He knows everything we know, including all our plans to expose him. No doubt he's on his way here right now.'

I had been such an idiot. But there was no time to feel sorry for myself. We had to act. 'Fine,' I said, snatching back Other Rabbit's head and body. 'He hasn't caught us yet. We'll just do the plan sooner. We split up, right now, all five of us run off in different directions and talk to the first grown-up we find. It's not late, there's probably still people in the park...'

But Vani and the others had stopped listening to me. They were listening to a different sound, listening wide-eyed, in a kind of a trance. I listened too, but I couldn't hear anything. For a few seconds there was complete silence. I strained my ears. And then I did hear it.

It was the tinkle of an approaching ice-cream van.

19

Greensleeves

It was the same tune I'd heard when the ice-cream van came to my house that night. Now, same as then, I didn't understand it. Why play music? Why let the people you're chasing know you're coming?

The answer was right in front of me. I had been frightened by the sound of the music, but it had the opposite effect on Vani's gang. They seemed completely calm, sitting there with silly smiles on their faces as if the ice-cream van held the answer to all the problems in the world. As the sound got closer, they became more and more relaxed. And then all four of them stood up and shuffled towards the boarded-over doorway like a procession of tiny zombies.

'Where are you going?' I asked. They ignored me, and started pulling the planks away from the door.

'What about my plan?' I said. 'We'll split up, yeah? Run away, in different directions.'

But they didn't go in different directions. Vani, William, Hannah and the other one whose name I didn't know all marched, single file, straight towards the music.

20

The One Whose Name I Didn't Know

I tried to stop them of course. I grabbed the one whose name I didn't know and twisted her around to look at me. 'What are you doing?' I asked. 'We should be running away.'

The girl didn't seem to hear me. She waited until I let go of her arm, then turned back towards the music and stooped to crawl outside. By now the other three had already gone. I didn't know what else to do so I jumped on the girl's back and flattened her.

'Sorry,' I said, 'but I had to do that. Are you OK?'

She didn't reply and she didn't try to shake me off. She just lay there, patiently waiting for me to get off her back. Outside the music was still playing. Vani, William and Hannah were probably at the van by now.

'Please,' I said to the one whose name I didn't know. 'Come with me. There's still time for us to get away.'

She didn't reply. This was pointless. The ice-cream men were probably on their way to get us right now. What was I going to do, pick the girl up and carry her?

I stood up, and the one whose name I didn't know crawled on through the gap into the park outside. I grabbed both bits of Other Rabbit, then followed the girl through the gap, stood up and ran as far and as fast as I could across the grass and away from the music. I didn't know what direction I was running in, or where I hoped to end up. I only knew that my new friends had been captured and that it was all my fault.

21

Cat Flap

Very early the next morning, as one end of the sky was turning pink, I was lying in a back garden looking at a cat flap, wondering if it was wide enough for me to fit through.

I tried to nudge the cat flap open with my head but it wouldn't budge. I pushed against it with my hands, then lay on my back and used both feet to try to kick it open. Still nothing. I was back on my feet looking for an open window when the flap made a quiet beep and a gingery cat slipped through from inside.

I worked out that it must be a special cat flap that only opens for one cat. This cat had a little black tag dangling from its collar: perhaps that was the secret to making it work.

The cat looked at me suspiciously. It seemed to know what I was planning to do next. It sneezed at me, then darted away as fast as it could. I charged after the cat, into a clump of prickly bushes and jumped up to grab its tail just as it tried to scramble over the fence into the next garden. I held on tight and pulled with all my weight until the cat lost its grip and fell back in a scratching, yowling mess on top of me.

It was a big cat and it put up quite a fight, but I managed to get onto its back and wrap my legs around it before its claws could do much damage. Once I got its collar off I let go, and the cat backed off, hissing. I think it was a bit embarrassed.

I looped the collar round my own neck and crawled back to the cat flap, which made the same beepy noise and let me though. Once Other Rabbit and I had squeezed through the hole, I could hear the cat trying to follow us, bumping its head against the flap, wondering why it wouldn't open.

I was in a kitchen. A big kitchen, with worktops all round the edges but another worktop in the middle, like on a TV cooking programme. You could tell rich people lived here.

I went upstairs. All the doors off the landing were closed and for a moment I was worried. How would I know which was the right bedroom? But it was soon obvious. Only one door had a skull and crossbones and a big sign saying 'Danger, do not enter.'

I entered.

The room was smelly. There were piles of clothes all over the floor and a bowl of dried-up cereal on the carpet next to the bed. The walls had posters of horror films and footballers.

What was the best way to do this? Grab him and shake him? Jump on top of the bed? No, that might make him scream and then his parents would come running. Better to do it gently. I pulled back the curtains and climbed up onto the windowsill. The sun was rising now, and the light on his face was enough to rouse him from sleep.

James the Babysitter opened his eyes and saw me.

'Hi James,' I said. 'Remember me?'

22

Two

James was still frightened of me; I could see that. He wanted to cry out for his mum and dad, but at the same time he didn't want to lose his cool. He didn't want to admit he was scared of a tiny girl.

He didn't say anything, so I spoke instead, trying to sound calm and confident. 'You're probably wondering how I got into your house aren't you, James?'

I was still wearing the cat's collar, so he possibly wasn't wondering that, but he still didn't say anything so I went on. 'I've come to you for help, James. You're the only hope I've got. If you tell any adults about me or phone the police, then I'll be taken away and you'll never see me again. But if you listen to what I have to say, then between us we could save my family.'

James kept on looking at me for a bit. Then he said, 'Go on'.

So I started telling him everything that had happened to me in the last few weeks. But as soon as I tried to arrange my thoughts I suddenly felt impossibly tired. It had taken about six hours for me to walk from Bramwell Gardens to James' house at the address I'd memorised and looked up on a map months earlier. I had been awake for nearly twenty-four hours now and for most of that time I had been either escaping, running, thinking, talking or wrestling a cat.

Now, in the warmth of James' bedroom, my body slumped forwards and I started to slide off the windowsill. James sat up in his bed and watched as I toppled over face-first into a pile of his stinking clothes.

Maybe I would have stayed there, lying face down in the pile until I suffocated to death on teenager stink, but James did finally get out of bed and help me up. 'You can have my bed,' he said. 'Mum never comes in here without my say-so. You'll be safe.'

Without even taking my shoes off, I climbed up, into James' still-toasty bed, the first bed I had been in since climbing out of my cot all those days ago. It smelled even worse than the clothes on the floor, but it was soft and comfortable. James laid the duvet over me like he was tucking me in, and as I sank into sleep I noticed the date on the clock by his bed. The fourteenth of September.

That date meant something to me. It took a moment to remember. Oh yes: today was my birthday. I was two.

23

Twelve Predicted Nines

I woke up to find a cup of orange juice and some slices of pizza next to the bed. The pizza was cold and plasticky, but delicious. The clock showed that it was still my birthday, but now around four in the afternoon. James was probably at school or college or wherever teenagers go during the day.

I walked over to the window and peered out. There was a car on the driveway meaning it was likely James' mum or dad was in the house. Better that I stayed in the bedroom until James got home.

I sat on the floor on the far side of James' bed, ready to hide if anyone did come in. I thought about my family. I thought about what might have happened to Vani and William and Hannah and the one whose name I didn't know. I wondered whether James' cat had managed to find its way inside.

I had arrived at James' house last night without a plan. All I knew was that I had to get away from Bramwell Gardens, away from the ice-cream van. I had considered sticking to Plan A and telling the nearest adult, but after what happened at the park, that felt like a bad idea. Vani and the others had been hypnotised and captured, and it was all my fault. I didn't want to do anything that might make the situation worse. I was determined to fix things by myself.

That meant James was my only option. For one thing he wasn't a proper grown-up. He was a teenager, which is kind of in-between being a kid and a grown-up. For another thing, he already knew the truth about me, and he hadn't told anyone so far, so that meant I could probably trust him, sort of.

And for a third thing, I remembered that Mum said he'd been predicted twelve nines in GCSE. I didn't know what that meant exactly, but it had something to do with being clever. Perhaps it meant he could help me plan what to do next.

The bedroom door opened. I lay down flat and rolled under the bed, clanking into a hard metal disc.

'It's me,' said James. 'You can come out.'

I rolled back out, rubbing my head.

'Yeah, that's my free weights,' said James. 'I work out sometimes.'

I didn't know what that sentence meant, so I just said, 'Thank you for the pizza.'

James nodded. 'Are you ready to explain yourself now?' he asked.

So again I explained things. It was less than twenty-four hours since I had told my story to Vani Patel, but since then there was lots more to add. I tried to explain it as clearly as possible without missing out any important details. I felt like I must be doing a good job because James didn't interrupt me once.

When I got to the end, past the part where I wrestled James' cat and fell off his windowsill, I sat back and waited for James' reaction. He thought about it all for a few moments, then said, 'So you never told anyone about me?'

'What?' I said. 'Told who? What are you talking about?'

'When I was babysitting at your house that time. You never told the government or the space lobsters. About me.'

'Space lobsters? James, have you even listened to a word I just said?'

'Yes,' said James. But he didn't look like he'd followed much of it.

'I thought you were supposed to be clever,' I said. 'I thought you had twelve predicted nines.'

'I *have* got twelve predicted nines,' said James, 'but they're in Maths and English and stuff, not... Freaky Weird Baby Conspiracy Studies.'

Great, I thought. So much for my hopes of James and me solving the problem together. All he cared about was keeping himself out of trouble.

'So I'm not in danger?' he said. 'No one's coming to get me?'

'No, James,' I sighed. 'No one's coming to get you. There are no space lobsters. The bad guys are after *me*, and they've already got my family and all of my friends. But you're completely safe.'

'Good,' said James, taking a phone out of his pocket. 'In that case, I'm going to hand you in.'

I panicked. 'What are you doing?'

'Phoning the police,' he said. 'It's for the best. For me, I mean. Not for you.'

I thought back to that night in my bedroom at home, when James had threatened to go to the newspapers. The only way to stop him had been to threaten him, so I did it again now.

'Fine,' I said. 'Ring the police. They'll come and take me away, and they'll take you too.'

'Why would they do that?'

'To cover their tracks. Think about it, James. My whole family disappeared. Mum, Dad, Lewis. Easy peasy. They'll make you disappear too, and your parents as well probably.'

'I don't believe you,' said James. He still had the phone in his hand but he hadn't dialled any numbers yet. 'They won't take me away. They'll probably thank me and give me a medal.'

It was time to take the threats up a notch. 'James,' I said. 'If the police take me away, I'll tell them you know *everything*. I'll tell them you're part of a big secret organisation and you're really dangerous.'

'But – that's not true!' whined James. 'I don't know everything! I don't know *anything*!' For a moment he looked like a little boy and I almost felt sorry for him.

James stayed quiet for a few moments. I think he was trying to work out something clever to say, but he obviously couldn't think of anything because all he finally said was, 'I really don't like you.'

'Don't blame me,' I said. 'You started all this. If you hadn't tried to steal Mum's credit card that day, I wouldn't have phoned the police, you wouldn't have seen me and I wouldn't have come to you now.'

To my surprise, James seemed to think this was a fair point. 'Yeah,' he said. 'I suppose.' He put his phone back in his pocket and I relaxed a little bit.

'I'm sorry I threatened you,' I said. 'Please can we trust each other and work as a team?'

'Not got much choice, have I?' he said. 'So, go on. What do you want me to do?'

That was an easy question to answer: 'First I'd like some more pizza, please.'

24

Next

James was right that no one ever went in his bedroom. He told me he had an arrangement with his mum: she went in there once a fortnight, stuffed his dirty clothes into a wash basket, hoovered up and opened the windows to let out the smell. Apart from that, the room was all his.

It was the perfect hiding place for me. Well, not perfect because of the smell, but it was definitely safe. It was a place for me to rest and to think. James brought me food – mostly crisps and orange juice – and I even persuaded him to go to Next and buy me some new clothes.

And once he got over the shock of me turning up, he became quite interested in my story. If he could help solve the mystery and save all the kids it would make him a hero and I think he liked the idea of that.

The other good thing about James was that, unlike me, he could walk down the street on his own without it looking weird, so he could go out and try to get some of my questions answered. The first place I sent him to was Bramwell Gardens, to get evidence of what had happened there. But he came back to tell me he hadn't found anything unusual. There was the old hall, and it had boarded-up doorways like I described, but there we no other clues or signs of life.

James had also been on something called Google Earth, on the Internet, to take a look at Forest Shades Holiday Village from the air. That wasn't much use. The trees made it impossible to see whether anyone was living there or not. He saw the lake in the middle, but no sign of any people.

Next, James bought a huge map of the United Kingdom, and stuck pins in it to show what he called the 'key locations' from my story: my house, Funkytots, Rumpus, Bramwell Gardens and Forest Shades. They were all quite close to each other so there was no need for him to have bought such an enormous map, but it seemed to make him happy.

'Look at the pins,' said James. 'See the pattern they make. What does that say to you?'

I looked at the wonky pattern. 'It doesn't say anything to me,' I said.

James looked disappointed. 'Me either,' he said. Then he perked up again: 'Listen to this.' He tapped the screen on his phone and a piece of music started up. I flinched the moment I heard it. 'That's it, right?' asked James. 'The ice-cream van tune?'

That's exactly what it was.

'Mr Close has engineered a Pavlovian response in the children, making them follow the tune whenever they hear it,' said James. 'That much is obvious.'

I didn't have a clue what he was on about.

'I downloaded the tune, the ice-cream van version,' said James. 'It's called Greensleeves. A traditional English folk ballad rumoured to have been written by King Henry VIII.'

'Right,' I said.

'What does that tell us?'

I thought hard. 'Nothing.'

'No,' he admitted. 'Me either.' With that he nodded sadly and his mum shouted him downstairs for his tea.

I thought James might have given up trying to

figure things out but the next afternoon he burst into the room again, full of excitement.

'I've got it!' he yelled. 'I can explain everything!'

25

Spies

'It's all about the pills!' James shouted.

'What pills?'

'When you were telling me about the other kids. Vani and that lot. They said Mr Close gave them pills every day. I bet that's what makes them clever.'

'Maybe,' I said. 'But that doesn't explain very much. It doesn't explain *me*. No one's been giving me any pills.'

'OK,' said James, looking a bit miffed. 'I didn't say I could explain *everything* did I?'

Actually he *did* say that but I decided not to remind him. 'So he's invented some pills that makes kids clever,' I said. 'But why do it in secret, in this weird holiday camp? Why not tell people about your invention and get rich?'

'That's the genius bit.'

I still didn't understand. I think that when James said, 'that's the genius bit' he meant that *he* was a genius for working it out.

'Please explain it to me,' I said.

'If you could invent the world's best spying machine,' said James, 'the last thing you would do is tell people. A spying machine only works if you keep it totally one hundred per cent secret.'

'So … these kids are inventing a spying machine?'

'No. These kids *are* spying machines. You, Vani, all of them. Look,' said James, 'imagine you were the head of a secret organisation. You'd want to spy on your enemies, yeah? Hide cameras, bugging devices, stuff like that?'

'I suppose so.'

'But that's really difficult. It's not easy to hide a spying device so it can't be found.'

I thought of the blinking light buried in Other Rabbit's neck. 'It's not that hard,' I said.

James ignored me. 'But imagine an actual human spy, hidden in plain sight. Two feet tall. With listening devices here…' James tweaked my nose. '…Cameras here.' He poked my eyes. 'And a super computer right here.' He patted me hard on the head.

'I still don't understand what you're talking about,' I said.

James sighed. 'I'm talking about *baby spies*. Say you're the prime minister of North Korea or something, yeah? You check your office for hidden cameras and bugs and it's all clear. So you start talking to your army generals, talking about where your weapons are hidden, whatever. Then in comes a little two-year-old kid. Say it's the cleaner's kid. No one bats an eyelid. You keep on talking like normal. No one sees the kid as a threat. Except *this* kid, right, *this* kid is remembering it all, storing it all in her tiny little superbrain, ready to file her report to the head of intelligence back in DC.'

James folded his arms and leaned back, waiting for me to admire his amazing mental powers.

I said, 'That sounds really stupid.'

'Oh, is it? Oh, sorry. Go on then, Chubbychops, let's hear your better idea.'

I thought about it. I didn't have a better idea. In fact James' theory kind of made sense. I thought back to all the secrets I'd seen and heard as a kid: Dad farting in the kitchen, the window cleaner peeing in his bucket, Kath eating baby food at Funkytots. They'd done those things like I hadn't been there at all, like I was invisible. Maybe I *was* a natural born spy after all.

James could see that he was beginning to convince me. 'You see, that's why they're so desperate to keep it secret. That's why they're after you. Once people know about the baby-spy programme it becomes useless.'

'In that case we should tell someone,' I said.

'No way!' said James. 'This is the government we're talking about! Not the normal government you see on the news but like the top-secret government who no one knows about.'

'So how do you know about them?'

James glanced around, as if someone might be listening in. 'It's all on the Internet,' he whispered.

'So, it's not very secret then.'

'Look, do you want my help or not?' said James irritably. 'I'm telling you: if you try to expose these people, they will destroy everything. The facility, all those kids, your family. They'll nuke it. And you and me too. Just to cover their own tracks.'

'You can't know that for certain,' I said.

'No,' he admitted. 'But do you want to risk it?'

That was a good question. Did I want to risk it? No. I didn't.

'OK James,' I said. 'Let's say I believe you. Let's say your baby-spy theory is true. And it's not safe for us to tell anyone. Say that's all true. What do you think we should do about it?'

'Glad you asked,' said James. 'I think you should make contact.'

26

Close Call

James' plan was simple. I don't think you could even call it a plan really. It was the only option we had. It wasn't safe to tell any grown-ups about me. And I couldn't keep living in James' bedroom forever because in a few days his mum was going to come in and tidy it. So what choice did we have? We had to get in contact with Mr Close and try to make some kind of a deal.

'Easy,' said James. 'All we have to do is ring him up.'

'On your phone? They can probably trace it.'

'Of *course* they can trace it. So we won't use my smartphone. We use a public telephone box. It takes forty seconds before you can triangulate someone's position from a public call.'

'Is that a true fact,' I asked, 'or did you learn it from a film?'

James looked grumpy again. 'It's a true fact, which I happened to learn from a film,' he said. 'I've located a candidate phone box. On an intersection of three major roads, giving us multiple opportunities for escape should the need arise.'

'That's great,' I said, 'but you're forgetting something. We don't have Mr Close's phone number.'

'I actually think we do,' said James. He dug into his pocket and pulled out the crumpled Forest Shades leaflet. On the back it said: *Start planning your dream getaway today. For all enquiries call: 0844 849 6126.*

We didn't make the phone call straight away. It was getting late, and it would have looked strange for me to be out and about at that time of night. We didn't want anyone to notice us.

So we waited and went out early the next morning. I had forgotten what it was like to walk down a street in daylight without having to hide from people. With James walking by my side I looked like a normal two-year-old out for a stroll with her big brother. Every time we crossed a road I told James to hold my hand. He wasn't happy about that, but we had to do it to look normal.

Finally we got to James' specially selected phone box. It was at a noisy road junction, but once we were inside with the door shut it wasn't so bad.

James took the telephone receiver and passed it down to me, then fed in some coins and carefully tapped in the number from the leaflet.

The phone rang for a long time. If you were calling a normal number you'd have given up and hung up. But I kept waiting.

After about three minutes there was a click and a voice came on the line. But not Mr Close. It was a woman's recorded voice.

'Thank you for calling Forest Shades. Unfortunately we are no longer accepting guests at this village, but please check our website for other exciting holiday locations across the UK.'

Then another click. Then a long silence.

James gave me a questioning look. I shrugged at him: nothing.

But I didn't hang up. The silence on the line sounded funny, like there was someone there, listening.

James looked anxiously at his watch. 'Forty-five seconds since connection,' he whispered. 'They might be triangulating our co-ordinates.'

I put my hand up to shush him. I spoke into the silence on the phone.

'Mr Close?' I said. 'Is that you?'

'Rita Jeffrey,' said the voice of Tiptoes the Clown. 'I wondered how long it would take you to contact me. I must say I have to admire your investigative...'

'Shut up,' I said. 'I'm talking, you're listening.'

Mr Close fell silent and I delivered the little speech that James and I had worked out in advance.

'I know all about you, Mr Close,' I said. 'I know what you're planning, I know what's going on with those kids, and that means I could blow your whole secret wide open any time I choose. So here's the deal. You let my family go. You let all those kids go, Vani and all the rest of them. If you don't do this within twenty-four hours, you will see me on the television news exposing your secret plans to the world.' I tried to seem as dangerous as possible. The threats sounded unconvincing in my piping two-year-old voice, and yet when I had said similar things to James, they had worked.

I waited for a reaction. James' eyes were flitting between his watch and the streets outside. I think he was expecting a fleet of ice-cream vans to come screeching round the corner at any minute.

'Is it my turn to speak now?' asked Mr Close.

'Go on.'

'Your proposition is very interesting, Rita. Here's my counter: if you don't present yourself at the front gates of Forest Shades within *twelve* hours, I'll kill your parents.'

And then he hung up.

27

Maccy D's

After Mr Close hung up on me, I tried to call him back. The number rang and rang and didn't even connect to the recorded message. After about five minutes of ringing, the phone simply went dead.

By now James was insisting that we get away from the phone box, in case the ice-cream men turned up. We went to Maccy D's, where he bought himself a Coke and got me a small milkshake, and we sat together in one of the booths.

James tapped at his phone. 'Forest Shades holiday village is forty miles away. Sixty minutes by car, or eleven hours on foot. So you've got time to walk there before he kills anyone.'

'Walk there?' I said. 'Why would I walk there? We'll take your parents' car. You can drive it to the facility, find a weak spot in the fence where we can smash through and...'

James put down his Coke. 'You are joking, right? I'm fifteen years old.'

'So?'

'You have to be seventeen to drive.'

I shrugged. 'Fifteen, seventeen, what's the difference?'

'Two years!' he shouted. Some of the other customers looked over at him so he pretended to relax and took a long, noisy suck of his drink. 'I'm not allowed to drive a car,' he whispered. 'Plus I don't know how. We wouldn't get past the end of the street.'

I thought back to my experience trying to steal the Porsche. Maybe James was right and it was too difficult. 'What about motorbikes?' I said. 'Can you ride one of them?'

'No.'

'Trucks? Tractors? What about a helicopter?'

'Look,' said James, 'it's not about whether I can drive or not. It's...' He looked a bit embarrassed. 'The thing is. I'm not coming with you.'

'Oh,' I said.

'It's not that I don't *want* to come,' said James. Then he went quiet for a few seconds.

'It *is* that you don't want to come,' I said, 'isn't it?'

James peered down his straw as if he was

inspecting a microscope. 'Yeah.'

I was disappointed in James but I understood. This was all my problem, not his. At this moment in time, Mr Close didn't even know James existed, and James wanted things to stay that way. I couldn't blame him.

But all the same, there was no way I was walking forty miles to Forest Shades Holiday Village. 'Eleven hours on foot means for a normal adult,' I told him. 'My legs are half as long, so it'd take me twice the time. My family would be dead before I got there.'

James thought about it. 'OK,' he said, 'how's this? I'll get the bus with you. I'll take you to within a couple of miles of the village, so you don't look strange travelling on your own. But then I'm turning round and coming home.'

'Thank you,' I said. 'But if you don't hear from me in the next two days, that's when you need to go to the police and tell them everything you know. OK?'

'Yeah, definitely,' said James. But as he said it he was tearing the plastic lid of his drink into strips and not looking at me. I knew that he was lying. If I didn't come back, he wouldn't do a thing about it.

28

Home, James

It took three different buses to get from James' house to an area near Forest Shades. The journey took hours. This gave me time to try to come up with some sort of plan. I would have liked to discuss my ideas with James along the way, but the buses were too busy and people would have heard our conversation, so I stared out of the window hugging Other Rabbit and thinking while James played games on his phone.

We got off the bus at a lonely stop next to a pub. No one else got off there. On one side of the road were farm fields, and on the other was a thick forest. A little bit further up the road, there was a turning off into the forest, with a sign pointing the way to Forest Shades Holiday Village. The road sign was dirty and bent at a weird angle. You could tell it had been a long time since any holidaymakers came this way.

'I'll walk you round the corner,' said James, 'until you're out of sight of the road. But that's it. Then I'm coming back to the other bus stop and going home.'

'Remember what I told you,' I said. 'If I'm not back in two days…'

'I remember,' said James. But he didn't make any promises.

We got to the turning and walked a little way along into the forest together. It was daytime but the tall trees blocked out most of the sunlight. The road was cracked, with weeds growing out through the tarmac. It didn't look like many people came down here.

James stopped. 'This is as far as I go,' he said. 'You're on your own now.' He was terrified. Even coming this far had been a pretty brave for him.

'Thanks for your help, James,' I said. And I meant it.

'Good luck, Rita.' He awkwardly shook my hand then turned to go, and it was a few seconds before I noticed he had called me by my name for the first time ever. I stood and watched him go all the way back to the main road, then waited another few minutes to give him time to catch the first of his buses home. I did this for two reasons. First, I wanted to make sure he was safely on his way home, and second, I wanted to make sure he hadn't realised that I'd dipped my hand into his coat pocket and stolen his mobile phone.

29

Welcome to Forest Shades Holiday Village

About a mile down the road there was another turning, onto an even narrower road, and another skew-wiffy sign pointing to the holiday village. I knew that I was close now, so I made my final preparations. I took out James' phone and tapped it awake. I had to put in a security code to make it work, but that was easy enough. I'd seen James do it plenty of times: 4827. Then I went into settings and turned the code off so I wouldn't have to enter it next time.

Next I tapped in the phone number I'd memorised, back in the staff room at Rumpus. The phone number from the newspaper, where it said: 'Got a story? Call our 24-hour hotline and leave a message.' I saved the number to the phone under the name HOTLINE.

I didn't press the CALL button yet, but I made

sure my fingers could do it without looking. Then I hid the phone.

I turned into the narrow road and walked on for a few minutes until I reached a high fence, running right across the roadway and blocking my path. Attached to the fence were signs saying 'Danger', 'Keep Out' and 'Private Property'. They reminded me of James' bedroom door. I wouldn't have been able to go any further except that a little hole had been cut in the fence, a hole just big enough for me to walk through. I squeezed through the gap and kept walking, until I got to a small building at the side of the road. Sticking out from the building was a yellow barrier like the ones they have on car parks to stop people getting in without paying.

I'd expected to see some guards by now. Uniformed soldiers with guns and fierce dogs, something like that. But since saying goodbye to James I hadn't seen another human being. I walked on underneath the yellow barrier without having to duck.

'Rita!' called a voice. 'Long time no see!'

It was a child's voice, and I recognised it. I turned to see him sitting inside the window of a little wooden hut.

'Hello, Hector,' I said.

Hector climbed up into the window frame and dropped outside to join me. He was wearing blue dungarees and a shiny silver badge that read PREFECT.

'Lovely to see you again,' said Hector. 'I'm sorry I wasn't entirely honest with you last time we met. Pretending to be on your side and so on. I'm sure you understand. Oh, and I'm also sorry I had to pop that tracking device into your bunny.'

He reached out and grabbed Other Rabbit from my grasp. A couple of days ago, I had borrowed a needle and thread from James and used them to carefully stitch Other Rabbit's head back on. Now Hector ripped it half-off again and stuffed his fingers down into Other Rabbit's foamy guts. 'But you have to admit,' he went on, 'a cuddly toy is an excellent place to hide a bug. Which is why I need to check that you aren't pulling the same stunt on me.'

Hector rummaged about until he was satisfied. 'All clear,' he smiled, handing my floppy-headed rabbit back to me. Luckily I had hidden the phone up inside the sleeve of my duffel coat.

'I'll need to check the rest of you for bugs as

well of course,' said Hector. 'Would you be so kind as to take off your duffel coat?'

I pretended to struggle with the buttons of my coat as I let the phone slip down, out of my sleeve and into the freshly ripped opening at the top of Other Rabbit's neck. Then I lay Other Rabbit on the ground and gave Hector my coat.

Hector ran his hands all around the coat. Satisfied it was empty, he told me to stand in a star shape while he patted my arms and legs, peered into my ears and mouth and finally ran his fingers through my hair like he was checking for nits.

'Good,' he said. 'I didn't think you'd be daft enough to wear a wire, but better safe than sorry.'

Hector handed my coat back. I slipped it on and casually picked up Other Rabbit. He felt heavier now, with James' phone hidden in his belly. I looked around. 'Where are the adults?' I asked.

'What adults?'

'I don't know, the guards.'

Hector shrugged. 'I'm the guard, if you want to call it that. It's my turn to man the gatehouse anyway. Not a difficult job to be honest. Hardly anyone tries to escape, and it's very rare for us to receive visitors.'

'There must be adults somewhere, Hector.'

'Says who?'

'Says me. I've *seen* them.'

Hector looked amused. 'Really? Which adults have you seen?'

'I saw Mr Close at Rumpus. I know he's also Tiptoes the Clown. I saw the ice-cream men...'

Hector interrupted: 'You *saw* the ice-cream men?'

I thought back to my encounters with the ice-cream men, at home and at Bramwell Gardens. 'Well, no, I didn't see them but I heard them.'

'Them? Plural?'

I didn't know what he was on about. 'I don't know what you're on about,' I said.

Hector kept looking at me and grinning. He was waiting for me to realise something. Finally, I did.

'You don't mean...' I said. 'You can't be telling me they're the same person. Mr Close, Tiptoes, the ice-cream man... Hector, are you telling me this whole place, this whole weird project is run by *one man*?'

'And what a guy,' said Hector. 'Just wait until you meet him properly.'

'But that's nuts! One man couldn't run this whole place by himself.'

Hector looked a little hurt. 'He doesn't do it by himself. We help him. Myself and the other prefects.'

'Oh well, that makes perfect sense then,' I said. I was being sarcastic, something I suppose I had picked up from James. 'The whole place is run by one man and a bunch of toddlers.'

'You should know by now,' said Hector. 'We're not ordinary toddlers. Watch.'

With that, Hector let out a sudden screech, leapt up in the air and kicked the yellow barrier. It snapped in half like a breadstick.

I tried not to let Hector see how scared I was. 'But why would you *want* to help Mr Close?' I cried. 'He's keeping you prisoner!'

'You've got the wrong idea about this place, Rita,' said Hector. 'It isn't a prison. Those people you met – Vani and the rest – they aren't representative of our community. Most of us love it here.'

Hector draped a friendly arm around my shoulders and gave me a tight squeeze. 'Right then,' he said. 'Shall we go and say hello to your parents?'

30

Mum and Dad

Past what Hector had called the gatehouse, the road carried on through the trees and into a car park. It was big enough for hundreds of cars, but now there was just a small blue car and an ice-cream van.

'We could walk the whole way,' said Hector, 'but these are probably quicker.'

At first I thought he meant the car and the van, but then Hector pointed me to a small fenced-off area containing five or six micro-scooters.

'Take your pick,' said Hector. 'You do scoot, I assume?'

I picked a bright yellow scooter and followed Hector as he zipped off out of the car park. Now the roads got narrower, as if they were meant for bicycles rather than cars. It was mostly downhill so after a couple of pushes Hector and I were sailing easily down the path, past rows of little lodges and into the heart of the holiday village. Back at James' I had spent hours studying the map of the village, hoping that when I arrived I would know my way round, but I was soon totally lost. I felt like we'd gone down the same roads two or three times and I wondered if Hector was doing this on purpose to make sure I got confused. For the whole journey we didn't see a single other person.

'Here we go,' said Hector, skidding to a stop. I had to swerve to avoid scooting into him, and I almost fell onto my face, but I managed to change it into a jump and make it look like I did it on purpose.

We had stopped in front of a lodge just like all the others, except this one had lights on inside and the grass around the front had recently been mown.

I was suddenly very frightened. 'So ... my mum and dad are in there?'

'And your brother, of course,' said Hector. 'We're all very fond of little Lucas.'

'Lewis,' I corrected him.

'That's the fella. Well, in you pop. They're expecting you.'

I walked up the red-brick path to the door. It was slightly open but I knocked anyway. 'Hello,' I called. 'It's me. It's Rita.'

I had a sudden thought, and turned back to Hector. 'Do they know about me?' I asked. 'I mean, do they know I'm clever? Will they expect me to act like a normal two-year-old, like I used to act, or…?'

'Don't worry about that,' smiled Hector. 'Be your lovely self.'

I pushed open the door and went inside. The telly was on, showing an old episode of *Britain's Got Talent*. I recognised it: there was an old man playing a xylophone while his wife tap-danced next to him.

I couldn't see Mum or Dad. Then I realised: I *could* see them. They were there, sitting very still on the sofa, watching the TV with a tube of Pringles on the table in front of them. Had they even noticed me come in?

'Mum,' I said. 'Dad, it's me.'

'Hello there, Rita,' said Dad. 'Come and sit up on my knee, we'll watch a bit of telly.' He didn't sound at all surprised to see me.

'Mum?'

'Hello, sweetie,' said Mum. She grabbed hold of me and gave me a kiss on the head, but she didn't take her eyes off the tap-dancing lady.

'Are you all right, Mum?' I asked. 'What happened to you?'

'Come and sit up on my knee,' Dad repeated. 'We'll watch a bit of telly.'

I turned to Hector, who had followed me inside. 'What have you done to my mum and dad?'

Before Hector could answer, a bedroom door crashed open, and something flew across the room and leapt on to my back, knocking Other Rabbit out of my hands.

'Ritaaaaaa!' shouted Lewis. His weight toppled me over onto the floor but I didn't care. At least someone was excited to see me.

'Lewis!' I shouted back. He was still clinging on to me like a backpack so I had to wriggle my fingers under his arms and tickle him loose. Lewis chuckled and rolled around on the carpet.

'How're you doing, Lulu?' I asked.

Lewis snarled at me. '*Don't* call me Lulu. *Don't* like it.'

'Sorry, buddy.' I'd called him Lulu on purpose, to see if it made him angry. It did make him angry and that was good because it meant that Lewis was still normal. Whatever they'd done to turn Mum and Dad into zombies, they seemed to have left my brother alone.

'Are you OK, Lewis?' I asked. 'Are they looking after you here?'

'Yeah,' said Lewis. 'There's a *massive* playground, and I can play Minecraft all day and they let me have Diet Coke.'

'That sounds great,' I said, before turning back to Hector and asking him again: 'What have you done to my mum and dad?'

'They're fine,' said Hector. 'Look, they're having a whale of a time.' Up on screen, the xylophonist and tap dancer had been replaced by a little girl singing a song from *The Greatest Showman*. Mum and Dad were staring at her with blank looks on their faces.

'You've hypnotised them,' I said. 'It's like the thing you do with the ice-cream music.'

'No, this is slightly different. Your parents are in a chemically induced state of passivity and suggestibility.'

155

'A what?'

'I'll demonstrate,' said Hector. 'Mr Jeffrey: tip those Pringles down your trousers please.'

'You're the boss,' said Dad. He stood up and tilted the tube of crisps so they slid into his pants. Then he sat down again with a slow crunch. I couldn't believe what I was seeing.

'Look, Rita,' said Hector. 'I'm not the best person to explain this to you. Why don't you come and meet Mr Close?'

'I think that's a good idea,' I said. 'See you later, Lewis. Behave yourself.' I reached out to tickle Lewis again and he ran giggling back into his bedroom.

I looked around for Other Rabbit and flinched a bit when I saw him dangling from Hector's hand. Trying to be calm, I took back my toy. Hector didn't resist. I risked a quick glance down: the phone was still in there inside Other Rabbit's stuffing. Hector hadn't noticed the extra weight.

'So where do we meet Mr Close?' I asked. 'In his secret laboratory? Or an underground bunker or what?'

'No actually,' said Hector. 'He thought Costa Coffee might be nice.'

31

Rats

It was a five-minute scoot up to Costa Coffee. This time we did see other people along the way. They were all children, none of them older than about four. Some were on scooters like ours, others were walking or on balance bikes. I didn't recognise any of them. One of them might have been William from Bramwell Gardens, but he scooted past before I could get a good look, and he showed no sign of recognising me.

In fact none of the kids we passed showed any interest in me. That seemed strange; I was a new face after all. It was like they were scared of me or, more likely I suppose, scared of Hector. None of them said hello to him either.

Costa Coffee was in a courtyard near a sign saying 'Village Square'. There was a Pizza Express, a shop called Fat Face and a few others. They were all closed and looked as if they'd been closed for a long time. Costa looked shut too, but there was a single light shining from behind the counter. As we got off our scooters and walked up to the door, a rat skittered across the bricks in front of me and disappeared into the bushes. Hector paid it no attention.

'Wait here a moment,' said Hector. 'I'll tell him you've arrived.'

Hector went inside, leaving me alone in the courtyard. This was a chance to put my plan into action. I turned my back to the window, pulled James' phone halfway out of Other Rabbit, woke the screen and pressed CALL to dial the number I had saved under HOTLINE. The battery was about half full and there was a strong enough phone signal for the call to connect. I could hear it ringing and then connecting at the other end.

'All systems go!' called Hector from behind me. I jumped and pushed the phone back down into Other Rabbit's guts, then turned to follow Hector into the darkened coffee shop. Whatever happened to me now, my story would finally make its way into the outside world. I only had to make sure Mr Close told me everything, as loudly and clearly as possible.

32

Babyccino

Mr Close was waiting for me behind the counter. 'Rita!' he called out. 'Welcome! I've been looking forward to this moment for so long! Please, take a seat, I'll get you a babyccino.'

He kept grinning across at me as he fussed with the different pipes and squirters on the coffee machine. You wouldn't think that less than a day earlier he had threatened to kill my parents.

'Thanks,' I said, 'but I'll just have a drink of water.' In front of the counter was a big basket filled with bottles of water, so I reached in and grabbed one.

'No!' yelled Mr Close. 'Not those!' I dropped the bottle and he quickly calmed down. 'Please, take a seat,' he said. 'Allow me to bring you some water, and perhaps a bite to eat too? Snack? Don't tell me: Pom Bears.'

I chose a seat at one of the dusty tables. Mr Close nodded at Hector, who went behind the counter and came back with three bags of Pom Bears. He brought them over to my table and tore them open for me. I was hungry, so I ate them. Without saying anything else, Hector backed off into the shadows.

Mr Close stepped out from behind the counter, carefully carrying a tray of drinks. A steaming black coffee for him, tap water and a babyccino for me. He put the tray down on the table and sat opposite me.

'So,' he said. 'Tell me, Rita. How did you do it?'

'Do what?' I asked.

'Do what, she says! The modesty of the girl! How did you manage to evade my devious clutches for so long? Where did you lie low?'

I shrugged. 'Here and there.'

Mr Close sipped his coffee. 'Did anybody help you out?' He asked this very casually but I knew that if I said yes and told him about James, Mr Close would go and track him down. I had promised not to drag James into this, so I shook my head. 'No one helped me,' I said, trying to sound tough. 'I did what you said, Mr Close. I

160

didn't tell anyone, and I came straight here. Now it's *your* turn to answer *my* questions, and then I want you to release my family.'

'Don't get your knickers in a twist!' said Mr Close. 'I'm just interested in you, Rita, that's all. You've done so remarkably well out there on your own in the big bad world. I'm proud of you!'

'What do you mean proud of me? Why would you be proud? You've got nothing to do with me.'

'I'm forgetting,' said Mr Close, with a creepy smile plastered over his face. 'You know so very little.'

He was seriously irritating me now, and I wanted to prove him wrong. 'I know all about this facility,' I snapped. 'I know how you give the kids special pills to make them clever and then train them so they can be spies.'

'Spies?' asked Mr Close.

'That's right. So you can go and spy on the president of North Korea and he'll think it's just a normal kid or the cleaner's kid or something and then…' I was repeating everything James had said to me, and even as I heard the words coming out of my mouth they already sounded dumb.

Mr Close listened patiently to what I was

saying, but not because he was taking me seriously. It was his way of making fun of me. This made me feel silly and angry, so I stopped talking about spies and said: 'I'll tell you one thing Mr Close; Tiptoes is a really rubbish clown.'

Mr Close tilted his head, like I'd made a fair point.

'So go on,' I said. 'Since you're so clever, go ahead and tell me what's going on. Explain what you're up to.' I shifted Other Rabbit up onto my knee to be sure that James' phone picked up what was coming next.

'All right,' said Mr Close. 'I'll start at the beginning.'

33

On Drugs

'For a number of years I worked for a large chemical company,' said Mr Close. 'You know the shampoo that doesn't sting your eyes? That was us. We made lipsticks, bath bombs, washing-up liquid, toilet cleaner, you name it. Half of the contents of your kitchen and bathroom came from our laboratories.'

Mr Close paused to take a loud slurp of coffee.

'But they also make medicines. Tons of the stuff. Antibiotics, antivirals, that gooey stuff you rub on your nostrils when you're bunged-up. They're always coming up with new pills and potions. And that's the bit where I worked, developing new drugs.'

I thought of Mum and Dad back in their little lodge, gawping at *Britain's Got Talent*. 'You mean, like the drugs you've given my parents?'

'Quite the opposite, actually. My team were developing a line of cognition enhancement supplements. Put more simply: clever pills. You know, take one tablet a day then learn Swahili before breakfast and finish *The Times* crossword in ten seconds flat. That sort of thing.'

'What's that got to do with you kidnapping my family and locking them up in an abandoned holiday village?'

'I'll get to that bit,' snapped Mr Close. He obviously wanted to tell his story in detail, and that was fine by me. I wanted the whole thing to be picked up by James' phone and recorded by the newspaper hotline. 'When you invent new drugs,' Mr Close went on, 'you have to test them. First you give them to mice, to see whether they drop down dead, and if they don't, you look for human subjects.'

It was starting to make little bit of sense. 'So you started feeding your pills to these children,' I said.

'No,' said Mr Close, irritated by my interruption. 'Please Rita, let me tell the story. We used adults. Paid volunteers at that. They'd come to the laboratory, take a pill, then try to solve some mathematics problems. And we tested whether the pills improved their performance. All standard procedure.'

The way Mr Close spoke reminded me of Hector, but then I released it was probably the other way round: Hector modelled himself on Mr Close.

'Unfortunately there was one small problem with the pills. Namely, they were rubbish. Didn't work. Test after test, not one jot or tittle of improvement in the subjects' intelligence. A total washout. Until: I noticed something interesting…'

Close stopped talking and stared at me until I asked: 'What did you notice?'

'I'll tell you! I noticed that the pills *did* have an effect – a very small effect mind you – on the very *youngest* adults. Our eighteen-to-twenty-four-year-old subjects absorbed new information significantly faster after taking the pills.'

Mr Close was getting excited now, leaning over the table towards me so that a fold of his tie dipped into his coffee. I suppose, living in this isolated holiday village, he didn't get to tell his story very often.

'This was a terrific breakthrough of course,' said Mr Close. 'It demonstrated that the pills weren't useless after all. They *did* work, but only on immature, developing brains.'

'You mean on kids,' I said.

'Exactly!' Mr Close sat up straight. The soggy bit of his tie sent a muddy stain spreading out across his shirt. 'The younger the subjects, the better the pills worked. This was an astonishing finding! And the obvious thing to do next was to test the pills on younger and younger children. Naturally I submitted this modest proposal to my supervisors immediately – but what did they do? Congratulate me? Give me a promotion? A pay rise? Not a bit of it! They closed down the whole experiment! Just when it was getting interesting!'

Close was getting angry now, as if I was the person who had stopped his fun.

'I asked my boss why she was pulling the plug and she blathered some nonsense about it being unethical to test powerful drugs on small children. Unethical! What does that word even *mean*, Rita?'

'I think it means it's the wrong way to behave.'

'You don't know what it means! Exactly my point. So of course I quit my job there and then. Marched out the door with nothing but my lab coat and laptop.' He paused for a moment and grinned at me. 'And of course a large plastic barrel full of clever pills.'

Mr Close sat back in his chair as if the story was over. But of course it wasn't. 'How did you end up in this holiday village?' I asked. 'Where did all the kids come from?'

'I'm coming to that,' said Mr Close. 'Once I resigned from my job, there was nothing stopping me. Fortunately I have substantial private resources, which enabled me to buy Forest Shades. This gave me the space and the privacy required to continue my research.'

'And where did the children come from?'

'Does it matter? I…' Mr Close waved his hand around, searching for the right word. 'I *acquired* them.'

'You mean you kidnapped them.'

'It isn't kidnapping when no one wants the children in the first place. I simply identified some reluctant parents, and we came to a financial arrangement.'

'You *bought* babies?'

'The children didn't seem to object.'

'How could they object?' I yelled. 'They were babies!'

'Well, they haven't complained since.'

'Maybe not,' I said, 'but they did climb over an electric fence to escape.'

Mr Close shrugged. 'Youthful curiosity. The grass is always greener on the other side of the electric fence, ha!'

I was pretty sure Mr Close had said enough now to get him put in prison. Everything he said had gone down the hotline to the newspaper. There might already be police cars speeding over here to arrest him. But I still hadn't asked my most important question.

'What has all this got to do with me?'

'Good question, Rita,' said Mr Close. 'For a long time I had no idea of your existence. In fact I came across you quite by accident, on a field trip.'

'A field trip?'

'I don't keep these children locked up all the time you know. Some of them can be trusted to come out into the big wide world with me every now and again.'

'The prefects,' I said.

'That's right, the prefects. You've met Hector, and there are several others too. I want them to learn about the world beyond these fences and so from time to time I take them out to show them a supermarket or a railway station or some such. Well, it was on one of these expeditions that one of my prefects – young girl called Evelyn – met you.'

I was shocked. She had met me? Surely I would have remembered.

'It was about two months ago,' said Mr Close, 'at another one of those awful soft-play centres. Apparently you toddled up to her and said hello and asked if she'd read all seven Harry Potters.'

I thought back to all the little kids I'd spoken to in my life. There were loads of them. I was always trying to find someone as clever as me but I didn't think I'd ever succeeded.

'Of course Evelyn played dumb,' said Mr Close. 'I'd trained her well. But she immediately came racing back to me and told me about what had happened. I couldn't believe my ears – another smart kid? It was impossible! Evelyn dragged me back to the spot where she'd encountered you, but you and your parents had already left. And so began the laborious process of tracking you down.'

'That's why you dressed up as a clown and came to my nursery.'

'Yours was the fifth nursery I'd been to!' said Mr Close. 'All I knew was that there was a clever little girl somewhere in the vicinity of that play centre. And so I came looking. Even then, I only located you once you started tapping information into your father's smartphone.'

My mind was swirling with all this new information. 'But hang on,' I said. 'You still haven't explained how I got to be clever without taking any of your brain pills.'

'Indeed I haven't,' said Mr Close. 'Because that was the last thing I worked out as well. I only fathomed it once I knew your name and the names of your parents. One of them rang a bell from my days at the laboratory, back when I was testing the pills on adults. That name was a Mrs Rebecca Jeffrey.'

My mum.

34

Snakes and Lizards

'But Mum isn't super intelligent,' I said. Come to think of it, Mum wasn't very intelligent at all.

'That's correct,' agreed Mr Close. 'The pills had no discernible effect on your mother's brainpower. But clearly they were still in her system when she fell pregnant with you. In other words, you took an immense prenatal dose of cognitive enhancement supplements.'

At last I had my answer. Two and a half years ago, when I was growing inside Mum's tummy, my brain was developing at top speed. And it was all because of Mr Close's pills.

Mr Close was still ranting on excitedly. 'You represent an incredible breakthrough, Rita! Previously I'd assumed this drug couldn't work before birth. But that's clearly not the case. I was a fool to assume! Just think where this research could take us next! Oh Rita, I'm so glad you've come home!'

That last word made me shudder. 'This isn't my home,' I said.

'Don't worry,' said Mr Close. 'You'll come to see it that way in time.'

'I won't! Never! And I won't work as a spy either!'

Mr Close sat back in his chair, puzzled. 'This spy business again. I really don't know where this idea of yours has come from. Spying has nothing to do with it.'

I believed him. Mr Close had been honest with me so far, so there was no reason for him to start lying now. I suddenly felt embarrassed. I wanted to blame James for his stupid spy theory, but Mr Close didn't know about James and I wanted to keep it that way. So I had to pretend it was all my idea.

'But if they aren't spies,' I said, 'then why are you making clever kids?'

Mr Close looked at me like he didn't understand the question. 'Why *not* make clever kids?' he said. 'Think about it Rita. Think about how much children *cost*.'

'They don't cost anything,' I said. 'Children are free. You're the only person who goes round buying them.'

'*A quarter of a million pounds*,' Mr Close yelled. 'Each! To feed it, clothe it, educate it to a standard where it can support itself. Quarter mill per kid! It's outrageous!'

I frowned. I was pretty sure Mum and Dad hadn't spent half a million pounds on me and Lewis.

'Now consider this,' said Mr Close, launching into another of his speeches, 'every animal on Earth has its offspring in roughly the same way. The baby is born, or hatches from its egg, and the parents hang around for a few weeks. They feed the infant, fight off predators, maybe indulge in a small amount of play, and that's it. The youngster is left to fend for itself. Take that rabbit of yours.'

Mr Close pointed at Other Rabbit. I flinched, but Other Rabbit just stared, keeping his secret safe. 'The mother rabbit,' Mr Close said, 'spends just five minutes a day with her litter, popping into the burrow with scraps of food. After one month she hops it, literally. Snakes and lizards abandon their nests before the eggs even *hatch*.'

'Why are you telling me about lizards?'

'Because snakes and lizards can *afford* to abandon their babies,' said Mr Close. 'Because the babies know how to look after themselves. Same with the rabbits and the eels and the pandas and the crabs and every other species on this planet, with one exception.'

'People,' I said.

'Bingo! Human children are *completely useless*. For two whole years they eat, they poo, they vomit and they keep the rest of us awake at night with their incessant bawling. And they cost a fortune in the process.' Mr Close took a long swig of his coffee. By now it had gone cold so he let it trickle back out of his mouth into the cup. Then he carried on talking as if nothing disgusting had happened. 'And that's only the financial cost, Rita. Look at the hours involved in caring for it and teaching it. In this country a child attends school for twelve years minimum, during which time it makes *no* contribution to the economy *whatsoever* and wastes hundreds of thousands of pounds in teachers' salaries. Am I the only person who sees this as a problem?'

'Yes,' I said.

Mr Close ignored me and kept talking.

'Imagine a better world. A world where a child could take a simple course of my brain pills to speed it through the developmental process. It could go to school at the age of one, and graduate from university six months later! You could sack nearly every teacher in Britain, and all the unemployed teachers could go out and get proper jobs, alongside the five year olds who no longer needed school! They could *work*! They could *contribute*! They could *make this country great*!'

Mr Close stared at me, waiting for a reply. I think he expected me to say he was a genius. Instead I told him, 'I think you're a total nut job.'

'You're wrong,' said Mr Close. 'I'm performing a great service to mankind. Future generations will rank my name above Jenner and Salk.'

I didn't recognise the names. 'Were they total nut jobs too?' I asked.

'Edward Jenner discovered the smallpox vaccine. Jonas Salk discovered the polio vaccine.'

'And what have you discovered?'

'Isn't it obvious, Rita?' spat Mr Close. 'Don't you see?' He stood up from his chair and spread his arms out wide. '*I've discovered a cure for childhood*!'

35

Hotline

I'd heard enough of this. I had put up with Mr Close's nonsense so far, keeping him talking so that the whole story could be sent down the hidden phone to the newspaper hotline. But I didn't want to spend any more time sitting here with this horrible, coffee-dribbling man. I wanted him to know that his whole evil plan was about to come crashing down.

So I told him. 'Mr Close. I'm very pleased to tell you that you have been wasting your time. Very soon you're going to be arrested and no more children are ever going to take any of your nasty pills.'

'What are you talking about, Rita?' asked Mr Close, calmly.

I tipped back Other Rabbit's head and dug James' mobile phone out of the fluff. The call to

HOTLINE was still connected, still picking up our conversation. 'This whole time,' I said, 'you've been talking not just to me, but to the hotline of a national newspaper. Tomorrow morning this story will be front-page news and you, Mr Close, will be in prison where you belong.'

'Is that so?' said Close. It was weird: he didn't look very surprised. He sat back down in his chair and began picking at his teeth with his little finger. 'Then I suppose there's nothing I can do. Perhaps you should invite this reporter of yours to come along and take photographs.'

That seemed like a strange thing to say. 'There's no reporter there,' I replied. 'I think it's just a machine recording the call.'

'No,' said Mr Close. 'I think you'll find there is someone there. Why not say hello to him?'

I had a strange feeling everything was about to go badly wrong. I put the phone to my ear. 'Hello,' I said.

'Hello Rita,' said Hector.

36

Scarper

I thought my brain was going to cave in. How had Hector got himself to the newspaper office? Twenty minutes ago he had been right next to me, handing me a bag of crisps.

'Yes, how *did* I get myself to the newspaper office?' asked Hector, as if he was reading my thoughts. At that same moment, Hector stepped out from behind the counter with a mobile phone pressed to his ear.

'Of course Hector *didn't* go to the newspaper,' explained Mr Close. 'What he *did* do was to borrow your phone when you weren't looking, bring up this hotline of yours and change the number so it called *our* phone instead.'

'I borrowed it back at your parents' lodge,' said Hector. 'Remember?'

I thought back. He must have done it when I

was wrestling and tickling Lewis. For those few moments Hector had had Other Rabbit all to himself. I'd thought Hector didn't know about the phone. I'd been wrong.

'You should have worked it out by now, Rita,' said Hector. 'I'm really very good at this sort of thing.'

I was hopping mad. I wanted to hit and bite and scratch Mr Close and Hector like a proper tantrummy two year old. I was angry with them, and I was angry with myself that my whole plan had come to nothing.

'You look disappointed,' said Mr Close. 'Well to be frank with you, Rita, so am I. I was rather hoping that when you heard my story, when you learned about what I'm trying to *achieve* here, that you'd come round to my way of thinking. I hoped that you'd reach down into that bunny's guts and cancel the phone call.'

Mr Close sighed. 'But you didn't do that. You chose not to understand. You chose not to trust me. So now I can't trust you either. Which means we'll have to deal with you somehow.'

'Not forgetting James, of course,' said Hector.

Mr Close frowned at Hector. 'James?'

'James Formby,' said Hector. 'Aged fifteen. Registered owner of Rita's mobile phone. We have to assume he's in cahoots with Rita and should be dealt with accordingly.' My heart sank; I hadn't even succeeded in protecting James.

Mr Close looked at me, offended. 'Rita, you distinctly assured me that no one had helped you out. You see, this is just further proof that you're not to be trusted.'

Mr Close shot a meaningful look over to Hector. Hector moved closer towards me. 'Rita, Rita, Rita,' said Mr Close. 'Whatever are we going to do with you?'

Now was the time for me to come up with a new plan. A genius new plan that would destroy Mr Close's schemes, free the children of Forest Shades and get me back home with my family. I thought as hard as I could.

I couldn't think of anything. So instead I picked up Mr Close's coffee mug, sloshed the cold drink into his face, whacked Hector on the head as hard as I could with the empty mug, jumped out of my chair and legged it full speed out the door of Costa Coffee.

37

The Tunnel

I ran and ran. Across the courtyard, down a footpath and out into the forest. I don't know what I was looking for. I knew that the village was surrounded by electric fences, but I had a crazy hope that I might somehow get away. Maybe I'd find a hole in the fence or a fallen tree like the one Vani had used to escape. Maybe Mr Close and Hector would give up on chasing me. Maybe it would turn out that James had called the police after all, and I'd be rescued by a huge noisy helicopter with sweeping spotlights and a dangling rope ladder.

But none of those things happened. Instead I stumbled round the forest, getting more tired and frightened with every step. No one popped up to help me. I did reach the fence, but it was just like Vani had described it: three fences, the middle one surrounded by electrocuted dead animals. And there were no fallen trees to bridge the gap.

Then I remembered James' phone. For a moment I was filled with excitement: I could ring 999, or dial the real hotline number and get help! But the feeling disappeared as soon as I reached down into Other Rabbit's stuffing. The phone wasn't there. In my panic I'd left it back on the table at Costa Coffee. For all I knew Mr Close had stamped it to pieces under his boot by now.

So I kept on wandering through the trees without a plan. And that's when I spotted the tunnel entrance. It was about two metres inside the inner fence: a circle-shaped hole in the ground covered over with fallen branches. I ran over to the fence and looked out onto the grass beyond. There, a few metres out on the other side, the tunnel opened into the field. That end wasn't even covered up.

It was my chance to escape. I didn't know who or what had dug this tunnel, but I knew I had to use it.

I ran to the opening and yanked aside the branches. The tunnel was wide enough for me to squeeze in and just about crawl along on my elbows and knees. The earth walls were scratchy but not so bad as to make me bleed. It was OK. I could be through it and out the other side in a couple of minutes.

Except that there was no other side. Instead of going all the way, the tunnel stopped after about two metres. It wasn't like the middle section had collapsed; it was like the middle section had never been there in the first place. Like the two separate ends had been dug out on purpose, as a trick to make someone crawl inside.

So I wasn't surprised when two small-but-strong hands grabbed my ankles and dragged me backwards out of the hole. And I wasn't surprised to find that the hands belonged to Hector.

38

The Fort

'Hello Rita,' Hector said cheerily, as he pulled me back into the light. 'I knew you'd climb in there sooner or later.'

'You dug that hole,' I said.

'Weeks ago,' said Hector. 'It's a handy way of catching anyone who tries to escape. I can either waste my energy chasing them all over the forest, or I can sit back and wait for them to climb into the hole.'

I looked up at Hector's smug face. There was a red mark on his forehead from where I had whacked him with the Costa coffee mug. A small victory, but it made me feel very slightly better.

'Time we were heading back, Rita,' he said.

'OK,' I said. 'I'll come quietly.'

'Perhaps you would,' said Hector. 'But unfortunately we've learned not to trust a single word you say.' Hector grabbed my left arm and twisted it up hard behind my back. He was very strong for a three-year-old; he'd be pretty strong for a twelve-year-old. The only way to stop my arm hurting was to move in exactly the direction Hector wanted, out of the forest and back towards Costa Coffee.

When we got near to the Village Square, Hector veered me off to one side, in the direction of the wide lake that lay in the middle of Forest Shades. We walked almost to the water's edge, and for a second I wondered if Hector was planning to drown me, but instead he marched me around the lake, past some tied-up rowing boats and into a sort of adventure playground. There was a zip wire and a tall scramble net and one of those swings with a big ropey circle where loads of you can swing at the same time.

Hector walked me past all of this equipment and up to the door of a wooden fortress. The fortress was about the size of a big garden shed, made of wooden posts with narrow window slits cut into two of the walls. The door had two padlocks dangling loose on the outside.

'In we go,' said Hector, finally letting go of my arm and opening the fortress door. I stepped inside. Hector followed. It took a moment for my eyes to adjust to the gloom, but I soon made out that Mr Close was in there, sitting on the floor waiting for me. Next to him was a bottle of drinking water and a small plastic case, the kind you'd use for a game of doctors and nurses. It was all very creepy.

'Hello again, Rita,' said Mr Close. 'Apologies for the choice of venue, but my reasons will become apparent. This place has served me well in the past.'

The walls of the fortress were covered in scratches, mostly around the windows, as if people had scrabbled to escape.

'Earlier, you asked me about the drugs I'd given to your parents,' said Mr Close. 'They're basically inhibitors. They erase some pre-existing neural networks but other than that they're harmless. They delete some memories but they don't cause lasting damage. Your parents will be able to learn everything back in a fairly short space of time.'

I looked down at Mr Close's plastic case. 'You're going to drug me as well aren't you?'

'That's right,' said Mr Close, smiling. 'But like I

186

say, you'll be completely fine. You'll forget the last few weeks but you'll retain the capacity to learn, and learn quickly. We'll soon have you rebooted and playing for our team.'

I looked back over my shoulder at the fortress door. It was still open but Hector was blocking the exit, smiling at me. There was no way out. Mr Close picked up the plastic case and threw it across to Hector. Hector flicked the latches and lifted the lid.

'Honestly, Rita,' said Mr Close, 'there's nothing for you to worry about. Look at it as a nice long nap. You must be tired after all.'

Hector took a syringe out of the case. It wasn't a sharp syringe like you'd use to give injections. It was one of those mouth ones, like Mum and Dad had used to feed me Calpol when I had a temperature.

'OK!' I yelled. 'You win! I'll be on your side and do everything you say!'

'That's exactly what will happen,' said Mr Close. 'Once you've taken your medicine.'

'You can't!' I shouted. 'You can't, because...' I was making this up as I went along '...because I know something you don't!'

Mr Close raised one eyebrow. 'Oh yes?' he said. 'What do you know that I don't?'

'There are others like me,' I said, lying. 'Other smart kids, still out there in the world.'

'No, there aren't,' said Mr Close. He was trying to sound confident. But I could tell he wasn't completely sure.

'There are seven of them,' I said. 'Seven brainy kids. And I can tell you their names.' By now there was a little bit of an idea forming in my head.

Mr Close motioned to Hector to put down his syringe. 'All right, Rita. Tell me the seven names.'

'I don't know them off the top of my head. But I've got all the details written down in James' phone.'

Mr Close gave me a look. The kind of look you'd give to someone showing you a rubbish magic trick, when you knew exactly how the trick was done. 'So what you're saying, Rita, is that I should take out that phone and hand it over to you.'

I nodded.

Mr Close reached into his jacket pocket, took out James' phone and handed it over to me. 'This is quite pathetic of you, Rita,' he said. 'You know and I know that you only wanted that phone so you could make an emergency phone call. And I only let you have the phone because I happen to know there is no signal here.'

He was right of course. The top corner of the phone said NO SIGNAL. But I didn't need a signal. Because I wasn't trying to making a call.

'So come on,' said Mr Close impatiently. 'Where are these so-called names?'

'I'm still searching,' I said. And it was true: I *was* still searching.

'I'm sorry, Rita,' said Mr Close, 'but my patience really is exhausted now. Hector, prime the syringe.' Mr Close picked up the bottle of water at his side and threw it across to Hector. Hector unscrewed the top and sucked water up into the syringe.

I understood now why Mr Close hadn't wanted me to drink that bottled water back in Costa Coffee. It wasn't normal water: it was drugged. That water was how he got his drugs into people.

As Hector filled his syringe, I kept tapping at James' phone, frantically searching for the thing I needed. It might not still be here for all I knew. James might have deleted it. I opened an app and typed in the first few letters…

An arm wrapped itself around my throat. Hector, grabbing hold of me from behind. I tried to clamp my mouth shut but Hector squeezed my face and my lips puckered open like a fish. Hector nudged the syringe into the corner of my mouth. 'Good night, Rita,' he said.

The phone was still in my hand, open on the MUSIC app. I tapped where it said PLAY, and I pressed it. Then I closed my eyes, waiting for the drug.

39

Knots

The music started playing. What had James called it? 'A traditional English folk ballad, rumoured to have been written by King Henry VIII.' I wondered if Henry VIII every knew it would end up being used to sell ice creams.

But the history of the tune didn't matter. What did matter was that Hector did not squirt the drugs into my mouth. Instead he released his grip on my throat and stood staring at James' phone, hypnotised by the music.

The tune did not have that effect on Mr Close. 'Hector,' he said. 'Take the phone back. Give it to me.'

Hector didn't move. Mr Close leant forward to grab the phone off me, so I quickly reached up and let it slide out of my hand through the narrow window of the fort and onto the soft ground outside. Hector immediately stood up and turned around to follow.

'Hector,' said Mr Close. 'Don't be silly. Come back here.'

Hector ignored him. Mr Close grabbed Hector's arm. Hector shook it off and walked towards the fortress door, following the music.

'Hector!' said Mr Close again. Again Hector ignored him. And that's when Mr Close made his big mistake. He grabbed Hector's legs, toppling him to the floor, and then climbed on top to stop Hector getting any further.

A week earlier, back in Bramwell Gardens, I had been in the same situation as Mr Close was in now, pinning down the one whose name I didn't know to stop her from following the ice-cream men. But there was one big difference. The one whose name I didn't know was just a kid. But Hector was a prefect. And the prefects knew fighting skills. I'd seen Hector kick a traffic barrier in half and I knew he wouldn't be held down by Mr Close.

For a moment Hector lay flat, with Mr Close lying on top of his legs. Then Hector jerked round his right elbow, ramming it into the side of Mr Close's head. Mr Close let out a squawk. He tried to pin Hector back to the floor but Hector kicked his little foot up between Mr Close's legs, heeling him sharply in the goolies. Mr Close made a sort of 'oof' noise and rolled away to one side, allowing Hector to calmly stand up and walk through the door of the fortress, out towards the still-playing phone outside.

I could see Mr Close wouldn't be out of action for long, but I only needed seconds. I followed Hector outside, and as soon as I was through the door I swung it shut and clicked both padlocks into place, trapping Mr Close inside.

Hector was now standing over the phone, making no attempt to touch it, completely captivated by the music.

'A relatively smart move, Rita. I concede that.' Mr Close was back on his feet, talking to me through the thin window of the fortress. 'But you haven't achieved anything. You do realise that?'

'Get used to living in a little room, Mr Close,' I said. 'It'll be nice and cosy in prison.'

Mr Close snorted. 'Oh, who cares whether I go to prison? It doesn't matter what happens to me.

I'm not important. What matters is the *science*. The cure for childhood!'

'Believe it or not, people *like* childhood,' I said. 'People like *kids*.'

'Yes and people like gerbils too,' replied Mr Close, 'but not for a quarter of a million pounds each. And if the British government don't want to use the pills I've invented, someone else will. China, Russia – I think it was you Rita who mentioned North Korea. And once these other economies start to over-perform and take over the world, will we still be so sentimental about our little puking kiddiwinks then? That's when a new era will dawn…'

I knew what Mr Close was doing. He was trying to keep me talking while the phone battery ran out. As soon as it died and the music stopped, Hector would wake up and I'd be in big trouble. I knelt down to look at the display: 15% battery remaining.

From out of the gloom, other kids were walking towards us, drawn by the music. I recognised a couple of them: Vani Patel and Hannah. They didn't even look at me. They were under whatever spell the ice-cream music was casting. One of the other girls was wearing blue dungarees and a PREFECT badge like Hector's, but for the time being she was just as harmless as he was.

The first thing I had to do was tie up the prefects. I knew that when the music stopped, they'd try to take back control. So I picked up James' phone and led the children down to the lake, where the rowing boats were tied up. Mr Close was still yakking on in the distance – 'time for us to put away childish things and fulfil our destinies' – but by the time we reached the water's edge I could barely hear him.

Keeping the music as close to Hector's ear as possible, I dragged a length of rope out from one of the boats and used it to tie Hector's hands behind his back, and ankles, then bind him to the hands and ankles of the other prefect. I had no idea how to tie proper knots, so I just tied *lots* of knots, looping and repeating them over and over until I was pretty sure Hector couldn't untangle them. Then I did the same with the girl prefect.

I was still tying the ropes when James' phone battery died and the music stopped. The kids all snapped out of it in an instant: Hector, the girl prefect and all the other children standing around us.

'What the blazes is going on?' barked Hector.

'Rita?' said Vani.

'Who are you?' said the girl prefect.

I ignored Hector and the girl prefect. To Vani and the others I just said: 'Come with me,' and I led them back up to the Village Square and into Costa Coffee. I thought there might be a phone charger in there and sure enough there was one plugged in behind the counter.

I connected James' phone and used the time it took recharging to tell Vani and the others what had happened. I kept my explanation as short as possible because I knew we were still in danger: there were prefects out there in the village who had not been within range of the music, and who would set Mr Close and Hector free if they found them.

Vani must have had loads of questions, but she didn't ask them yet. The questions could wait. Instead we focused on what needed to be done right now. And as soon as the phone battery was charged, we did it. We went back out into the village as a team, with me leading the way and holding the phone out in front of me like a weapon. Whenever Vani pointed out a prefect, I pressed PLAY and led the hypnotised kid back to join the others at the lakeside. It would have been useful if Vani could have helped me tie the knots, but of course whenever the music was playing, *all* the kids went into trances. So I had to do the tying-up part on my own.

It took about an hour. By the time it was over, we had all the kids in one place, including the six prefects: a squirming bundle of powerless bullies.

It was proper night time by now. There were no outdoor lights in Forest Shades so it was difficult for us to see each other.

Vani took me to one side. 'Shouldn't the police be here by now?' she asked.

I suddenly felt embarrassed. I hadn't phoned the police yet. An hour ago I'd been standing in Costa with a fully charged phone and a strong signal, and I hadn't even thought about phoning them. How could I have been so forgetful?

Then I realised. I hadn't been forgetful. Without really thinking about it I had made a decision.

'We don't want the police to come here yet,' I said. 'First we have to destroy all the evidence of what Mr Close has been doing.'

Vani looked puzzled. 'I don't know much about the police,' she said, 'but I thought if they were going to put someone in prison, they needed to have evidence. Why would we destroy it?'

'Because,' I said, 'Mr Close was right. If people find out what's happened here, if they find out about his brain pills, they might use them. They might continue his work. We can't let that happen. We have to make sure that all of his work, every pill and laptop and scrap of paper, is destroyed.'

'And how are we meant to do that?' asked Vani.

I looked at her and at the group of three- and four-year-olds standing around her. 'You're a bunch of kids, aren't you?' I said. 'Well then, act like it.'

40

Kids Go Free

For the next two hours, the children of Forest Shades Holiday Village went bananas. They ransacked Mr Close's lodge and offices and ripped every piece of paper to shreds. They rowed his laptop computers out into the middle of the lake and dropped them overboard. They collected every single brain pill and ground them up into dust, then built a fire and sprinkled the dust on top. They also emptied Mr Close's wardrobes and dressed the trees with his shirts and jackets, which wasn't really necessary but seemed to make the children happy.

I would have liked to join in the fun, but I had some other jobs to do instead. The last job involved dragging a heavy plastic bin liner into the adventure playground, up to the padlocked fortress.

The fortress was quiet. Mr Close was not scrabbling at the walls or howling to be released. It was so quiet that I wondered if he had somehow managed to escape, but when I stood on my tiptoes at the narrow window, I could just about see that he was back in his original position, sitting in the corner.

'Hello,' I said.

Mr Close jumped in fright.

'Rita. What's happening? I heard children's laughter. I don't like that noise; it worried me.'

'I came to let you know,' I said. 'We're all going now.'

'Going? But – what about me? Are the police coming?'

'Yes,' I said. 'The police will definitely be coming. When I phone them. In a week or two.'

Mr Close laughed, but not like he found it funny. 'Two weeks? I'll starve to death by then. You'll have murdered me, Rita.'

'No, I won't. You'll be fine,' I said. 'Look: I've brought you a picnic.'

I posted thirty packets of crisps through the narrow window, followed by lots of sandwiches and pasta salads I'd found back at Costa.

'What am I supposed to drink?'

'I'm glad you asked me that,' I said. And I posted bottle after bottle of the drugged water through the slit, onto the pile of food inside. 'Don't gulp it all down at once.'

I couldn't really see Mr Close's face but I like to think it had a horrified expression. 'Rita,' he gasped. 'You can't expect me to drink this.'

'Why not? It's harmless.'

'*Harmless*?'

'It's a basic neuro-inhibitor to erase ... brainial networks,' I said. I wanted to repeat the exact words Mr Close had used to me earlier, but I couldn't remember them. But I think he got the point.

'But Rita, you don't understand! Your parents are on a carefully controlled dose. They can be back to normal in no time. If I drink this stuff for a fortnight it'll wipe me out completely! I'll regress to the level of a child!'

I stuffed the empty plastic bag through the window. 'This bag might be handy too,' I said. 'For rubbish and, you know, as a toilet.'

'Rita, please! My brain is priceless! Its contents could save humanity! Rita, you have to understand me!'

After that Mr Close said a lot more things, but I didn't listen and his voice got fainter as I left the playground. I went to pick up my scooter from the village square then scooted up to the place where the kids had all arranged to meet in the car park.

The small blue car was still there, next to the ice-cream van. Most of the kids were waiting around the side of the van as if they were buying ice creams, but of course the van didn't contain any ice creams. Instead it contained Hector and five other snarling, tied-up prefects.

I jumped off my scooter and walked to the front of the van to talk to the driver. 'Are you OK, Dad?' I asked him. 'Nearly ready to go?'

'You're the boss, Rita,' he replied, still with that same drugged-up look on his face.

'Seat belt on, Mum" I said. 'And you, Lewis.'

Mum buckled up, then fastened Lewis in between her and Dad. 'I get to go in the front!' squealed Lewis.

'That's right, buddy,' I smiled.

'Mr Jeffrey,' came a voice from the back of the van. It was Hector. 'Mr Jeffrey, would you pop round here and untie me please, there's a good chap.'

Dad unbuckled his seatbelt, ready to do as he was told. 'No Dad,' I said.

'Come on, Mr Jeffrey, be a sport,' called Hector.

Dad looked at me. Hector continued to call through, and for a few moments Dad looked like he didn't know which one of us to obey. Then he relaxed, smiled at me. 'You're the boss, Rita,' he said. And he rebuckled his seatbelt.

I walked round to the other children waiting outside the van. 'Get yourselves into pairs,' I said. 'You can't all stay together, but you can keep one friend each.'

'Where are we going?' asked Vani.

'For a long drive,' I said. 'We'll be driving all night, up and down the country. Every so often we'll stop near police stations and you'll get out, in your pairs. You'll go to the police, and when they ask where you've come from, you'll act dumb. Act like little kids, and don't tell them anything. The police will find places for you to go.'

'What about the prefects?' asked Vani.

'We'll do the same thing with them,' I said, 'except one-by-one, not in pairs.'

'But … they were with Mr Close. They're on his side. What if they tell the truth about this place?'

I smiled. 'They won't tell. That was Mr Close's first rule, remember: never talk to grown-ups. And so what if they *do* tell? They don't know how any of the science works. They'll just be freaky smart kids telling a crazy story. They won't achieve anything.'

Vani looked doubtful. 'Shouldn't we give them some druggy water first,' she said, 'just to be safe?'

I shook my head. 'No water. There's been enough messing with people's brains around here. That whole thing stops now.' I thought for a second. 'Actually,' I admitted, 'It doesn't stop quite yet. Dad,' I yelled, 'hit it!'

'You're the boss, Rita!' Dad pressed a button on the dashboard and the ice-cream van started playing its tune. Vani and the rest trooped into the back of the van, squeezing in alongside the roped-up prefects. They were as quiet as mice. I got in behind them and pulled the door closed, and Dad drove the tinkling ice-cream van out of Forest Shades Holiday Village and on into the night.

41

The News

The ice-cream van exploded in the middle of a farmer's field at six thirty the next morning.

It might sound like a dramatic way to get rid of a van, and I suppose it was, but after we had dropped off the kids, prefects and all, I got worried that someone might have taken down the registration number. If the ice-cream van was found and the police took fingerprints from it, maybe they'd identify Mum and Dad and take them in for questioning. It was too risky, so as soon as we were quite near to home I told Dad to drive off the road and into the field. I had a box of matches left by the kid who'd burned the ground-up pills, and I used the matches to set fire to the seats. The material was old and tattered so it caught fire quite easily.

I thought the ice-cream van would take a few

hours to burn, so it was quite a surprise when the whole thing went up in a massive, noisy fireball. But by then we were well out of danger, walking along a country lane towards our house.

***

Over the next two weeks, two stories appeared on the TV news:

First there was the news story about lots of young children found abandoned at police stations across the country, all on the same night. The children were too young to be able to explain how they had got there, so the whole thing was a mystery. The children were put in foster care and given the chance to start new lives with new families.

Then a week and a bit later there was the strange story of the Forest Shades lunatic. After receiving an anonymous phone call, the police arrived at an abandoned holiday village and discovered a man locked inside a wooden fortress on the adventure playground, surrounded by empty crisp packets and empty plastic water bottles. The man was healthy but completely unable to tell the police what his name was or why he was there. One policewoman said it was 'like talking to a two-year-old boy'. The man was later identified as the former research scientist Dr David Close. Dr Close was admitted to hospital for rehabilitation with a view to being released at the earliest opportunity.

***

Of course there were lots of other stories in the news over those two weeks, so no one made a connection between those two stories in particular. And that was fine by me.

There was a third story too, but this one wasn't on the news. This was the story of the Jeffrey family, who returned to their home early one morning after almost three weeks away. They got back to find a FOR SALE sign planted in the front garden, but it turned out that the estate agent and phone number on the sign were fake. The key in Mr Jeffrey's pocket still fitted the front door, and all of the family's belongings were still inside, packed into cardboard boxes.

Mr and Mrs Jeffrey, still under the influence of

Mr Close's drugs, happily unpacked their boxes and got on with life as if nothing strange had happened. And over the next few days, as the drugs wore off, things gradually went back to normal. They became a normal family again, with a normal four-year-old son and a normal two-year-old daughter.

If Mum and Dad had any sense that something weird had gone on, they didn't show it. Even when I heard Dad on the phone to his boss, trying to explain why he hadn't been to work in the last three weeks, he didn't say anything about getting kidnapped or drugged. He just said he'd been under the weather and forgot to phone in sick.

The only thing that rattled my parents was when Lewis kept asking if we could go back into the woods, where they had Minecraft and Diet Coke. Then Mum and Dad would look uncomfortable, as if Lewis had reminded them of a bad dream. They'd tell him to stop being silly, and quickly get back to whatever they'd been doing.

And me? I got on with my two-year-old life. I went to Funkytots and Rumpus with Other Rabbit under my arm, and sat in the shopping trolley with my feet dangling through, grabbing at biscuits as Mum pushed me along the aisles of Tesco. I did see Tim the guard give me an odd look, but I don't think he could be sure it was me. Anyway he didn't say anything.

As far as I can tell, the rest of the kids from Forest Shades are keeping quiet too, even the prefects. All we have to do is sit tight, act stupid, and wait to grow up. In another ten years, we'll be normal. They'll just have to make sure they stay away from any ice-cream vans because if they hear Greensleeves they'll go all weird and start trying to climb in the back.

Actually. When I say I've kept quiet, that's not completely true is it? For one thing, I've written this book. When I got back home from Forest Shades, Mum and Dad were still woozy for a few days, so it wasn't a problem for me to sit in front of Mum's laptop and type up everything that had happened.

And now I'm going to email it off to a publishing company. I'll tell them it's a made-up story. They can get any old bozo to pretend they wrote it. But at least I'll know my story is out there, and that'll be enough for me.

And from now on I'm going to behave myself. Well, more or less. I'll put James' phone in an envelope and post it back to his house with a thank-you note. I might borrow Mum's credit card and use it to send James a big bottle of vodka. I might phone the RSPCA too and report our local vicar for kicking his dog, and email the local newspaper about what goes in the window cleaner's bucket. But I'm allowed to get up to a little bit of mischief, aren't I?

After all, I'm only a kid.

Also from Firefly

The Lori and Max books by Catherine O'Flynn

Lori and Max

Longlisted for the Branford Boase Award 2020

Times Children's Book of the Week

Longlisted for the Blue Peter Book Award 2020

Lori wants to be a detective but, so far, the most exciting mystery she has solved is the disappearance of her nan's specs down the back of the sofa. Max is the new girl at school and Lori is asked to look after her. Max is a bit weird. She doesn't fit in – but then neither does Lori really.

When both Max and some money go missing, Lori is the only person who doesn't think Max has stolen the cash and run away. Even the police don't want to investigate. Suddenly Lori finds it's down to her to solve a real crime.

'A wittily told detective story about two eccentric and endearing girls – it's a real page-turner.' **Jacqueline Wilson**

£6.99 | ISBN 9781913102029

Lori and Max and the Book Thieves

Times Children's Book of the Week

A stolen phone, an unruly dog, a buried lunchbox and an antique children's book. Lori and Max must dig through layers of lies to solve two mysteries.

Lori and Max and the Book Thieves follows the two resourceful school friends as they look out for mysteries, injustices and high-quality confectionery in their neighbourhood. Funny, warm-hearted and beautifully written, this is the second in a MG crime series that shows the everyday heroics of friendship and family.

'...packed full of twists and turns ... I devoured it in one sitting... Another compelling and thoughtful tale that is bound to delight mystery lovers.' **Jo Clarke, @bookloverjo**

£6.99 | ISBN 9781913102357

The Alex Sparrow series by Jennifer Killick

Alex Sparrow and the Really Big Stink
Selected for the Summer Reading Challenge 2017
Longlisted for the Shrewsbury Big Book Award 2018

Alex Sparrow is a super-agent in training. He is also a human
lie-detector. Working with Jess, who can communicate with
animals, they must find out why their friends – and enemies
– are all changing into polite and well-behaved pupils. And
exactly who is behind it all.

Alex Sparrow and the Really Big Stink is full of farts, jokes and
superhero references. Oh, and a rather clever goldfish called
Bob. In a world where kids' flaws and peculiarities are being
erased out of existence, Alex and Jess must rely on what makes
them different to save the day.

'A brilliantly bonkers, side-splitting, superhero story.'
M.G. Leonard

£6.99 | ISBN 9781910080566

Alex Sparrow and the Furry Fury
Selected for the Summer Reading Challenge 2018
#PrimarySchoolBookClub pick June 2018

Catching the school's runaway guinea pigs is not really giving Alex job satisfaction, but how can he find a bigger test for his and Jess's awkward superpowers? Jess is more worried about the bullied new boy, whose Mum runs the local animal sanctuary. To befriend him she gets a voluntary job there, but she soon realises that something is very wrong; the animals are terrified. People start reporting strange events: things missing, property destroyed, and the local squirrels have turned mean. The police have no suspects. It looks more and more like a job for Agent Alex...

'Cracking adventure full of daft stunts, villainous villains and one far-too-cute hedgehog.' **James Nicol**

£6.99 | ISBN 9781910080740

Alex Sparrow and the Zumbie Apocalypse

The Zumbies are on the rampage – members of the Cherry Tree Lane Zumba class are apparently dying and then mysteriously coming back to life! Alex, Jess and Dave have to put a stop to it before Alex's mum and nan join the living Zumba dead or there'll be no family Christmas.

But why are the Zumbies curiously drawn to the Christmas lights? What does the Octopus sign mean? And who is the evil genius behind it all?

£6.99 | ISBN 9781913102043

At Firefly we care very much about the environment and our responsibility to it. Many of our stories, such as this one, involve the natural world, our place in it and what we can all do to help it, and us, survive the challenges of the climate emergency. Go to our website www.fireflypress.co.uk to find more of our great stories that focus on the environment, like *The Territory*, *Aubrey and the Terrible Ladybirds*, *The Song that Sings Us* and *My Name is River*.

As a Wales-based publisher we are also very proud the beautiful natural places, plants and animals in our country on the western side of Great Britain.

We are always looking at reducing our impact on the environment, including our carbon footprint and the materials we use, and are taking part in UK-wide publishing initiatives to improve this wherever we can.